LAUGHS

Funny Stories

SELECTED BY
CLAIRE MACKAY

Tundra Books

10/98

© 1997 Claire Mackay

Published in Canada by Tundra Books, 481 University Avenue, Toronto,
Ontario M5G 2E9

Published in the United States by Tundra Books of Northern New York,
P.O. Box 1030, Plattsburg, N.Y. 12901

Library of Congress Catalog Number: 96-61148

All rights reserved. The use of any part of this publication reproduced,
transmitted in any form or by any means, electronic, mechanical, photocopying, recording, or otherwise, or stored in a retrieval system, without
the prior written consent of the publisher – or, in case of photocopying or
other reprographic copying, a licence from the Canadian Copyright
Licensing Agency – is an infringement of the copyright law.

Canadian Cataloguing in Publication Data

Main entry under title:

   Laughs: funny stories

ISBN 0-88776-393-6

1. Wit and humor, Juvenile. 2. Children's stories, Canadian (English).*
I. Mackay, Claire, 1930–

PS8375.L37 1997   jC817'.5408'09282   C96-931667-4
PZ8.7.La 1997

The publisher has applied funds from its Canada Council block grant for
1997 toward the editing and production of this book.

Cover illustration by Loris Lesynski

Text design by Laura Brady

Printed and bound in Canada

01 00 99 98 97   5 4 3 2 1

SC
LAUGHS

To my husband Jack, who has made me laugh for forty-seven years.

Special thanks to Camilla Gryski, aka Posy the Therapeutic Clown, who provided up-to-date research on the biochemical aspects of laughter.

CONTENTS

Laughing Matters

CLAIRE MACKAY

Few species laugh. We do. Some apes and chimps do, but only if you tickle them. Mind you, Jean Little – who has a story in this book – swears that her first guide dog, Zephyr, often played a simple trick on her, and then gave it all away by wagging his tail. And there is also the Cheshire Cat of *Alice's Adventures in Wonderland*, who slowly vanished until only his smile remained, but that terrible floating smirk has always scared me to death. (Besides, as a young man named Frank, who I met in the public library, told me: "Cats don't laugh. They snicker behind your back.") Only the human animal – you and I and maybe your brother – can laugh at a joke, or tell a funny story.

Laughing is one of the first things we do. After being born (which is, believe me, not a big knee-slapper for those concerned), after learning the tricks of breathing, eating as much as possible at all times, and burping, we laugh. Or at least smile. Small humans smile when they're a couple of weeks old, chuckle at a month – and laugh out loud a few weeks later.

When we're really little, we laugh at peek-a-boo games, weird sounds, and funny faces. Once we reach kindergarten, we laugh at comical drawings and cartoons, at nonsense rhymes, and at physical jokes like slipping on a banana peel, or getting a coconut cream pie right in the face – if they happen to somebody else. And when we learn language, a whole universe of humor opens up. We learn, for example, that the funniest letter in the alphabet is the sixteenth, and the funniest word is "underwear."

Laughing is also one of the easiest things to do. It's a reflex, something we do without thinking. When you go to the doctor, sometimes she hits your knee with a little hammer, and your foot jumps forward and kicks her in the stomach – which is pretty funny, now I come to think of it. That's a reflex act by your quadriceps muscle, and it tells the doctor that your nerves are in good shape. It's the same with laughing. It takes a few more muscles to do it, fifteen altogether, including the *risorius* – a Latin word that means "laughing" – and the *zygomaticus*, a muscle that lifts your upper lip, and when you do it, it tells everybody that your whole self is in good shape. (When you frown, on the other hand, it takes forty-three separate muscles, and you look terrible.)

Some people say laughing is a luxury reflex, because it doesn't really help humans to survive. Now that really makes me laugh. I say they're wrong. Nuts. No light in the attic. One sandwich short of a picnic. Without laughter, I think the human race would be extinct. Just a bunch of fossils who died young and grumpy. It's our safety valve, our way of getting rid of worry and anger, and it's a social, and sociable, act. (If you laugh only when you're all by yourself, you may need professional help.)

Laughing, finally, is one of the healthiest things we do. Scientists have found out that when we laugh, our brains release a chemical that makes us feel good all over and also builds up our immune system. Laughter may be the best medicine in the world. A writer named Norman Cousins certainly thought so: he wrote a book a few years ago, entitled *Anatomy of an Illness*. He was one sick puppy at the time, with a couple of painful diseases. The doctors gave up. So he went to his local library and got some joke books, and to his local video store and rented some comedies, and then went home and read the books and watched the films. He laughed and laughed and laughed. And in a few months he was well. (One of his favorite movies, and one of mine, is the Marx Brothers classic *Animal Crackers*, in which Groucho tells this joke: "I once shot an elephant in my pajamas. How he got into my pajamas I'll never know.")

Laughter is a gift of nature. Those who can make us laugh are gifted, too. They share that gift in this book, with jokes, wordplay, nonsense, slapstick, irreverence, wit and, above all, with a great sense of fun.

So – take two pages every four hours. Or whenever you need to. You'll feel better.

The Clark Beans Man

TIM WYNNE-JONES

The night before Dwight started at a new school, his mother asked him to make a list of things he was proud of about himself. The list started off okay:

1. Can do excellent Donald Duck impression.
2. Memorized the names, positions and jersey numbers of every player on the Toronto Maple Leafs hockey team.
3. Draws monsters that make Vanessa cry.

That was as far as Dwight got.

"I'm sure you can name fifty other qualities about yourself," said his mother.

"Like what?" said Dwight. But she didn't have time to tell him right then, and besides, it was time for bed. He had a big day tomorrow.

So Dwight drew a monster to scare Vanessa with. It worked, but it wasn't very satisfying, since she cried all the time anyway. Dwight's mother reminded him that Vanessa was also starting at a new school the next morning and that he might be a little more considerate.

Miss Milliken put Dwight in the second row from the window near the back. She suggested that Nancy could show him where they were in their math book. Nancy didn't hear her. She seemed to be interested in something going on outside the window, so Dwight was forced to clear his throat and say excuse me a couple of times.

"One hundred!" said Nancy.

"Thank you," said Dwight, turning to page 100.

"What?" said Nancy, turning to look at him. And then before he could say anything, she gasped, turned bright red and swore under her breath. One little word. Four times.

Dwight touched his face, as if maybe it was covered with marmalade or something.

Then the girl behind him leaned forward and told him they were on page 230, not page 100. The girl was giggling.

"What's going on?" said Dwight, looking over at Nancy.

"She was counting convertibles," said the girl. "It's a game we play. When you count to a hundred convertibles, the next boy you see is the one you're going to marry."

Speechless, Dwight looked over at Nancy. Her face, still crimson, was buried in her math.

"Is there any problem, Dwight?" asked Miss Milliken.

"No," he said. Except for the fact that he'd been in class fifteen minutes and he was already *engaged*.

In English later that morning, Nancy was asked to stand up and recite a poem the class was learning. It was written by William Wordsworth.

"I wandered lonely as a cloud," said Nancy, but as far as Dwight was concerned, she might have been wandering lonely as a bottle of cream soda. "I wandered lonely as a bottle of cream soda, that floats on high . . ." To Dwight she didn't sound as if she was walking through a beautiful meadow filled with daffodils. She sounded as if she was sauntering through a mall.

"Good," said Miss Milliken enthusiastically when

Nancy had finished. "You may add twenty-four lines to your bar graph, Nancy."

Nancy turned to the back of her English notebook and quickly topped up her bar graph. Dwight watched with some interest. Nancy had drawn a graph like a thermometer with a big star around 100. Apparently they had to memorize one hundred lines of poetry. Nancy was at forty-four.

Miss Milliken read another poem by William Wordsworth. It was called "The World Is Too Much with Us." It was a sonnet. Miss Milliken explained what a sonnet was, that there were fourteen lines in all and that in a sonnet like the one Wordsworth wrote there were eight lines in the first part and six lines in the second. She explained the rhyming scheme and that kind of thing. Dwight already knew about sonnets. It was good on your first day to find something you already knew.

Then Miss Milliken said everyone had to memorize "The World Is Too Much with Us" as part of their required memorization. Everyone groaned.

"You have a week," she said. The groans only grew louder. Undaunted, Miss Milliken continued, "I know the language is a bit strange to your ears, but it won't be once you've come to know it better."

The groans crescendoed and one big guy fell to the floor as if mortally wounded. Everyone laughed, including Miss Milliken. "Poetry never killed anyone," she said.

Dwight joined in the big groan session but just to be one of the class. Then a little guy near the front shot his hand up in the air.

"Yes, Kenny?" said Miss Milliken.

"I've been thinking," he said. "Can we learn more than a hundred lines of poetry? Can we learn as many as we want?"

"Oh, as many as you want. Yes," said Miss Milliken.

"Yes!" said Dwight under his breath. Nancy heard him and glared. She sure didn't want to marry someone who actually liked memorizing poetry.

"Because," said Kenny, leaning over his notepaper, scribbling away with a pencil, "if each blue line on the page represents two lines of poetry, you could get about sixty lines up the page, and if each bar was only about half an inch wide, you could get about ten bars across the page. You could graph about six hundred lines on just one page."

Everyone groaned again and said things like "Right, Kenny," and "Here he goes again," and "Make it hard for us, Kenny," and things like that. But they seemed completely used to this kind of outburst from him.

Everyone but Dwight. He stared across the classroom at the guy making calculations in his notebook while everyone poked fun at him. A little tiny guy with the strangest croaky voice. The voice reminded Dwight of something Vanessa had made with a scrap piece of old lumber. She'd hammered a million nails into it and dolled it up with some aluminum foil and a rubber band and called it a boat. Kenny's voice was like that, a weird little boat. Full of purpose.

Then it was recess. Kenny came right up to Dwight in the schoolyard. (He came right up to about Dwight's shoulder.)

"We play two-handed touch football," he said. It was sort of like an order. "You can be on my team."

Dwight said yes and the game started. They used a peewee-sized football, which seemed fitting because it was Kenny's ball. It was also Kenny's game, as far as Dwight could tell. Kenny's rules, too. Nobody seemed to mind except a big bear of a guy named Howie. The guy who had been mortally wounded by poetry.

"Get a life!" Howie would yell, just about every time Kenny made a pronouncement.

It was Howie who was guarding Dwight when Kenny unleashed a mighty throw down the sideline.

"I got it," yelled Howie, hurling himself at the ball. But the ball landed comfortably in Dwight's hands, and Howie landed not so comfortably on the chain-link fence.

"Run!" yelled Kenny in his nails-and-aluminum-foil-and-rubber-band voice. But Dwight wasn't sure if he should.

Howie groaned as if in pain.

"Are you hurt?"

"Forget about him!" screamed Kenny. "What are you doing? Run! Are you crazy?"

Suddenly Howie, still on the ground, kicked out savagely and smashed Dwight square in the knee. "Gotcha," he said, grinning ferociously. Dwight buckled from the kick.

Kenny arrived on the scene, breathless. "Give me the ball," he demanded. Dwight tossed him the ball, glad to be rid of it.

"It's dead," said Howie.

"Touchdown," yelled Kenny as he crossed the line.

"The ball's dead!" yelled Howie. "I touched him, you freak."

Kenny ran back. "It's two-*hand*ed touch," he said. "Not one-*foot*ed touch."

"Get a life, moron!" yelled Howie.

Then Howie and Kenny yelled at each other and pushed each other until the bell. The rest of the teams wandered off, but Dwight watched with interest. Kenny came up to about Howie's chest, but he didn't seem bothered by the big guy.

The game resumed at lunch and in the afternoon

recess. So did the argument. Howie was huge and dangerous looking. It amazed Dwight to watch Kenny take him on. Like a little Jack Russell terrier, yipping and nipping at a bear.

Dwight walked home through the park, reading Wordsworth's sonnet – he already had the first eight lines pretty well down pat. With his head in the book, he didn't see the bear until he walked right into him.

"Whatcha doing in my park?" said Howie.

Dwight was so surprised, he actually believed for a second that he had somehow wandered lonely as a cloud into someone's backyard. Howie made a grab for him, and Dwight danced out of his way, losing his English book as he did. It fluttered to the ground. Howie slid into the book as if it was second base, just as Dwight picked it up again. He got a scrape on the hand from Howie's foot and got away with another kick on the leg.

Lying on the ground, Howie laughed, as if he had won some kind of contest. This was his game and his rules. Dwight ran the rest of the way home. The first eight lines of the poem got all jiggled up in his brain, and it took quite a while to sort them out again.

He didn't tell anyone about the attack, but he drew a great monster with fat lips and too many arms and jack-hammer legs. Vanessa hated it so much that she tore it up in little pieces. Which was fine with Dwight.

The next day, Dwight approached Miss Milliken when the class was dismissed for lunch.

"When can we recite 'The World Is Too Much with Us?'" he asked, quietly so no one passing by would hear.

Miss Milliken smiled delightedly. "It's not due until next week."

"How about right now?" said Dwight. It wasn't a poem he planned on holding on to, if he could help it. And he wasn't going to recite in class any poem that had the line: "This sea that bares her bosom to the moon."

Miss Milliken sat down and crossed her hands. "Shoot," she said.

Dwight recited the poem.

"Word perfect," said Miss Milliken. From the satisfied little look on her face, Dwight gathered that she liked Wordsworth more than he did.

"So I can start my bar graph?" he asked.

"You certainly may."

"Do I have to learn the cloud poem the class already did?"

"Not really," said Miss Milliken. "But I doubt it would present you with much trouble."

"No," said Dwight. "No trouble. But if we can learn anything we like, it seems pretty short to me."

Miss Milliken chuckled. "Well, at last Kenny Finnigan is going to have some serious competition."

"I've got some catch-up to do."

"True," said Miss Milliken.

"But at least I beat him with this one," said Dwight proudly.

"Almost," said Miss Milliken. "Kenny was in first thing this morning."

They played touch football at lunch and then at recess. It was Kenny's ball and Kenny was always captain and he always chose Dwight. He chose him first, though there were much better players. He never chose Howie. He liked to yell at Howie. He liked to yell at everyone, but it was more fun yelling at someone when they were on the other team.

Kenny could pass the ball a long way, considering his size. He would kind of coil himself up like a spring and launch the thing with his whole body.

"Go long!" he'd yell at his teammates in his croaky voice. "Go long!" To Kenny, every play was a must play – the last chance to score. Every play was in danger of being interrupted by the bell.

Dwight was so busy staying out of Howie's way that he flubbed a lot of catches that day. He didn't say anything about what had happened in the park, but it was on his mind. He couldn't tell if it was on Howie's mind. It was hard to tell if anything was on Howie's mind.

That afternoon, Miss Milliken announced to the class that although they still had most of a week to get their poem memorized, two students had learned it overnight. She didn't say who. Everybody assumed Kenny, and, by a process of elimination, the rumor mills soon pegged "the new kid" as the other likely suspect. Nancy, at least, was convinced it was him. So was Howie, who shoved his finger down his throat a few times to show Dwight what he thought of kids who learned poems overnight.

And Kenny was convinced. He stared across the classroom with new interest in Dwight.

When the class had a free work time that afternoon, Kenny wandered back to Dwight's desk. When Nancy saw him coming, she turned away in disgust. "Oh, my *gawd*," she murmured.

"What's wrong with her?" Kenny asked, leaning on Dwight's desk.

Dwight shrugged.

"Oh, my *gawd*," said Nancy.

But Kenny wasn't really interested in Nancy. He hunched forward and lowered his voice. "What are you doing next?" he asked.

"What do you mean?"

"Get off the pot!" said Kenny. He had such a gleam in his eye, Dwight gave up trying to pretend he wasn't the phantom memorizer.

"I dunno," he said.

"Come on," said Kenny, smiling a crooked smile. "You tell me and I'll tell you."

But Dwight didn't know yet and he said so.

Kenny looked hard at him. Dwight didn't blink. Kenny sighed. "If that's the way you want it," he said. "But this means war."

After school Kenny caught up to Dwight walking east along Gladstone. He tapped him on the shoulder and Dwight jumped out of his skin.

"Nervous, eh?" said Kenny.

"You just surprised me."

"Huh!" said Kenny. "You're scared. Admit it."

Dwight was. And he was just about to tell Kenny about Howie's attack in the park when Kenny suddenly burst out, "Okay, okay. I'll tell you what I'm learning: 'The Charge of the Light Brigade.' Ever heard of it?"

Dwight shook his head, momentarily confused.

Kenny smiled wickedly.

"*'Theirs not to make reply,*
Theirs not to reason why,
Theirs but to do and die.
Into the valley of Death
Rode the six hundred.'"

"Fifty-five lines in all," he said. "Beat that!"

Dwight lost his nerve. How could he explain to someone like Kenny that he was afraid of Howie? Kenny – all two foot nothing of him – was fearless. At football. At memorization. At everything.

They parted at Fairmont, and Dwight headed south, but he didn't take the opportunity to peruse his English textbook for large poems. He kept his eyes peeled for large bear-like boys with large bear-like tempers and small worm-like brains.

He got almost all the way across the park before Howie got him – got him from behind. He'd been lying in wait. He jumped out of the bushes and tackled Dwight with a shout of glee.

"Leave me alone," said Dwight, writhing on the ground, trying to get himself free.

"Leave me alone," aped Howie, sitting on Dwight's chest, pinning his arms down with his knees. Dwight gave up and lay on the hard ground, waiting for whatever was going to happen next.

"This is for pushing me in the fence," he said. He made a big horking noise.

"I didn't push you in the fence," said Dwight. He turned his face away just as a huge gob of spit landed on his cheek.

Howie's laughter was cut short, however, because suddenly there was a kamikaze scream from behind them and a peewee football came hurtling through the air and hit Howie square on the back of the head.

"Hey!" said Howie, losing his grip on Dwight, who immediately started to struggle free.

Kenny came running towards them and scooped up the ball where it was bouncing around on the ground.

"Get off him, you big fat lummox," he yelled, and beaned Howie with the football again.

"Cut it out," yelled Howie, covering his head with his hands. Dwight dragged himself out from under Howie, who was clambering to his feet.

Meanwhile, Kenny had retrieved the ball again. "Catch," he said, and he threw it at Howie, who caught it.

"Throw it back," said Kenny, jumping about like a crazy target.

"You stupid nerd-for-brains," yelled Howie. But –

and Dwight couldn't exactly understand this – he threw the ball back to Kenny.

Kenny immediately took his quarterback stance.

"Go long!" he yelled. "Go long!"

"Forget it," said Howie.

"*Go long!*" shouted Kenny, and there was an urgency in his voice, as if it was the last chance in the game and they were one touchdown behind and it was all up to Howie to save the day. Dwight turned in amazement to watch Howie suddenly take off, fading long down the field: twenty, thirty, forty yards, waiting for the big bomb that would win the day.

"Are you okay?" muttered Kenny under his breath.

"Yes," said Dwight, wiping the spit off his face.

"Get ready to run," he said. For Howie had stopped, realizing, too late, that he'd been had.

"Now!" said Kenny. And, tucking the ball into his pocket, he started running, with Dwight beside him, leaving Howie ranting with rage like some gullible giant in a fairy tale.

They tore down a path that skirted the playing field until they came to a concrete tunnel through the hillside. It was dark and the ground was muddy. They splashed on through. On the other side, Kenny veered suddenly off the track and up the steep slope into the trees, with Dwight right behind him. He was pretty sure Howie hadn't followed, but he was running now for the sheer exhilaration of escape.

They came out of the wooded hillside at a narrow street of little houses, out of breath from the climb, but still not ready to quit the adventure. Halfway down the block, Kenny once more veered down an alley. He was five strides ahead of Dwight when he cut behind a dumpster that sat out back of a long, low office building. Out of view, they stopped at last, panting heavily, and leaned against the yellow brick wall of the building.

"Thanks," said Dwight, when he could speak again.

Kenny smiled triumphantly. "I started thinking about how jumpy you were," he said between big breaths. "Then I figured out which way you went home and I thought, ah-ha! – Howie!"

"Amazing," said Dwight.

"No," said Kenny. "Experience. He used to get me in that park, too."

For some reason, Dwight was surprised to hear of Howie intimidating Kenny, let alone beating him up.

Kenny pulled a stick of Juicy Fruit from his jacket pocket. He fished around for another one.

"Where do you live?" he asked. Dwight told him. They were almost neighbors. Then Kenny told him how to get home without going through the park. He used the stick of Juicy Fruit like a conductor's baton, as if he was drawing the way home in the air. Dwight watched the little yellow baton and listened carefully.

There was no more gum in Kenny's pocket, so he tore the one stick in half.

"There are two kinds of bullies," he said, handing one half stick of gum to Dwight. "The kind who beat you up in the schoolyard for attention, and the kind who beat you up in secret."

Dwight unwrapped his half piece of gum thoughtfully. "Howie's the second kind," he said. "He only shoves a bit at school and acts tough."

"Right," said Kenny. "The secret ones are dangerous."

They chewed in silence for a minute.

"He doesn't bug you now," said Dwight.

Kenny nodded.

"You've got to think of something – some kind of diversion – with a guy like Howie," he said. "I read somewhere that the movie director, Steven Spielberg, kept getting beat up by this bully at his school. Spielberg made movies even when he was a kid. So he went up to this bully one day and asked him if he'd star in his next flick. The bully said yes and became the hero of the movie. And that was that. They became friends."

"Cool," said Dwight.

"I tried it with Howie."

"You did?"

Kenny nodded. "Yup. He liked the idea of being a movie star. There was only one problem."

"What?"

"I didn't know how to make a movie."

"Oh," said Dwight.

"I didn't have a camera. No story, not even an idea – nothing."

"So what did you do?"

"I started taking the other way home."

The sweet taste of the gum that had filled Dwight's mouth seemed to wear off pretty quickly. Only half a stick. What could you expect?

"It worked anyway," said Kenny. "Well, kind of. While he thought he was going to be a movie star, he didn't beat me up anymore. It kind of broke the pattern."

"But when he found out –?"

"He never really found out. I mean, I never actually told him I *wasn't* going to make a movie. I just started taking the other way home."

Dwight thought of Howie in the park waiting day after day for Kenny to come. He tried hard to imagine a kid as stupid as Howie.

"The thing is," said Kenny, "he's going to get you every day in the park until you're not there to get.

But once he doesn't get you for a few days, he'll probably forget about it. Or find somebody else."

Dwight nodded. Then he sighed. He had dared to hope that cocky little Kenny could teach him how to stop Howie from bugging him. Not just how to avoid him.

Kenny clapped Dwight on the arm. He had a cracked kind of smile on his face. "Good things happen when you take a different way home," he said. "I'd never have found this place if I hadn't been trying to get away from Howie."

"This place?" Dwight looked up at the wall he was leaning against. It had just been a good wall to lean on until then.

"Come here," said Kenny.

He dragged Dwight along a bit until they came to a large window. The lights were on inside. They looked down into a basement room with a tiled floor and brightly painted walls. An art room. They leaned against the glass. A man inside was drawing at a big drawing table. Behind him there was a door with a red light over it. On the light were the words "ON AIR." The light was on. It was a studio of some kind.

"Threshold Studios," said Kenny. "They make cartoons."

The artist was painting a little man in a sailor suit. Dwight had seen the cartoon man before. It was the

Clark Beans man from the commercials on TV. Beside the artist was a thick wad of pencil drawings of the Clark Beans man.

When the artist paused in his painting, Kenny tapped on the glass.

The man looked up. He smiled and waved at Kenny. He got up from the table and stretched. He placed his paint brush carefully in a water glass. He came over to the window, waved at Dwight. Dwight waved back.

Then the artist took a thick marker from his pocket and wrote on the glass in big comic book-style letters, "Hi ya, guys. How yez doin'?" He turned the question mark into a worm with his head pointing down, recoiling in horror at the period underneath him, which was a hungry-looking face with big teeth. That period was going to eat the wiggly part of the question mark right up. The boys laughed.

To Dwight, the most remarkable thing was that in order for them to read the words, the artist had to write backwards, and yet it didn't seem to slow him down at all. Dwight was convinced that he was in the presence of a genius.

And the show wasn't over yet. The artist went over to his desk and grabbed the thick wad of pencil drawings. He held them up to the window and flicked them so that the little Clark Beans man seemed to pick up a spoon as big as himself and dig into a bowl of beans. The artist did the flip book a couple of times. Then he got a second one from beside his desk and flipped the pages in it. Now the Clark Beans man was pole-vaulting right over the bowl. Well, almost. He didn't make it and landed KERSPLASH! in the middle of the beans. It was brilliant.

The boys clapped. The artist bowed and waved goodbye, pointing at his watch and making chopping gestures at his neck. He was going to get it bad if he didn't get the Clark Beans job finished soon. He went back to work.

The boys leaned against the glass and watched him for about a year. Luckily, time stood still, so their parents didn't report them missing, and they didn't get hungry or anything. Not much happened, really. The Clark Beans man gained a blue shirt and a painted-on smile. Then another artist came in to discuss something, and that broke the spell. They could leave.

When Kenny and Dwight went their separate ways at the end of the block, Dwight made his way home thinking that getting beat up had almost been worth it.

Almost.

He took Kenny's advice for the rest of the week and walked home the long way around the park. Howie never said anything about it at school. It was just as Kenny had predicted. It was as if Howie didn't even think about beating you up if you weren't there. Or maybe it was only when he was in the park that something came over him.

One day after school, Dwight went to the public library and asked the librarian for a book with some good poems in it – adventures, if there were any. They found a book of narrative poems that had "The Charge of the Light Brigade" in it, so Dwight settled down with that.

He liked "The Charge of the Light Brigade." It was exciting. But then he found "The Shooting of Dan McGrew" by Robert Service and, as far as he was concerned, it was better. For one thing it took place in the Yukon. But, most important, it was fifty-eight lines long – three lines longer than Kenny's poem. He started learning it right away.

Kenny was already at 80 lines on his bar graph, and "The Charge" would take him up to 135. So Dwight decided to learn "The Cremation of Sam McGee" as well. It was also by Robert Service. It was 68 lines long, with eight lines thrown in for free because the first bit got repeated at the end. Along with the Wordsworth sonnet, he'd be up to 140. Kenny might have had a head start, but that only made Dwight work harder.

When he recited "The Shooting" one morning before class, he asked Miss Milliken not to tell Kenny; he wanted it to be a surprise.

Very carefully he colored in the rising mercury on the poetry thermometer at the back of his notebook. He'd done the Wordsworth in red because he was thinking of the bar graph as a thermometer. But he decided now to do each poem in a different color. He did "The Shooting" in black. And he was going to do "The Cremation" in fire-bright orange!

He recited "The Shooting" on the Monday of his second week at school. He spent the long way home working on "The Cremation." By the end of the week he wanted to be neck and neck with Kenny.

When Dwight stopped to think about it later, he wasn't really sure why he walked through the park the next day after school. He hadn't forgotten about Howie. But Howie, apart from yelling a lot when they were playing ball at recess, didn't seem so dangerous anymore. Partly it was that. But partly it was also that Dwight was angry at having to go the long way home. He had dropped by Threshold Studios a couple of times and the artist always said hi and drew little cartoons on the window, if he had the time. It was great. But Dwight wanted to *choose* how he got home. So on Tuesday, he chose to go home by the park. He was faster than Howie. It would all be fine as long as he was prepared.

It was a sunny day. The park looked empty. Dwight walked quickly, keeping his eyes on the bushes where Howie had surprised him before. He glanced around a few times to make sure Howie wasn't sneaking up on him.

He was most of the way across the playground when he heard a car door slam. He looked over. Somebody had stopped to let off a passenger. The passenger was Howie. He waved at Dwight, as if they were friends. Were they? Or was it just a show for the driver of the car? His mother, perhaps.

"Oh, Mom, there's my new pal Dwight. Mind if I walk the rest of the way home?"

Dwight waved back but he didn't stop. Just a little wave. It was possible. He wanted to believe it was possible. They only lived a block apart. They played football together every recess. What's more, Kenny had said all you had to do with someone like Howie was break the pattern.

"Hey, wait up," called Howie.

Dwight slowed down a little. Friends? It made sense

to have someone like Howie as a friend rather than as an enemy.

Howie was getting closer, lumbering over in a kind of friendly way, not racing over with his fists clenched. Was it possible?

"Hi, Howie," he called out. Then he saw the bear look back toward the road. The car was out of sight. And when Howie turned back toward Dwight, there was nothing like friendliness on his face.

It was too late to make a run for it. Dwight tried, but again Howie tackled him. Dwight hit him with his books a couple of times, but that only made the bear growl. Howie took Dwight's books and hurled them away. Then he sat astride Dwight's chest and pinned his arms to the ground with his knees.

He laughed. "Tricked you," he said. "Just like you nerd-for-brains tricked me!"

Flicking his index finger with his thumb, Howie pinged Dwight in the forehead.

"Ow!"

"That's for tricking me," he said.

"I didn't trick you," said Dwight.

"And here's sixteen more, one for every line of that stupid poem."

"Ow! Ow!"

Howie laughed like a maniac.

Dwight was furious. "Stop!" he shouted. "You're going too far!"

"Why should I?" said Howie.

"Because there are only *fourteen* lines in a sonnet, you idiot!"

Howie stopped, but not because he cared about how many lines there were in a sonnet. Dwight had made a mistake, a whole bunch of mistakes. Daring to cross the park had been his first mistake. Thinking that maybe Howie and he could be friends had been his second mistake. And calling Howie an idiot had been his last mistake. Without Howie saying a single word, Dwight could see in his eyes that he'd gone too far. He could feel Howie's anger turning to stone on his chest. There wasn't anything he could do.

Or was there?

Had he gone too far? Or had he just not gone far enough?

"Only fourteen, you idiot!" he shouted again. But this time he shouted it in the voice of Donald Duck.

Howie looked at him in amazement.

"Jeez! Don't you know nothin' about poetry, you crazy, good-for-nothin' excuse for a stump!"

Howie was looking at him strangely. Strangely wasn't the same as nastily. And so with great force and with the only muscle not pinned down by the hulking body of Howie the bear, Dwight began to recite Wordsworth's "The World Is Too Much with Us" in the voice of Donald Duck.

Howie was transfixed. Transfixiated. Rendered motionless. In all his years of beating up nerds, no one had ever recited poetry to him in the voice of Donald Duck.

Dwight could feel the body over him relax. But it wasn't until he started "The Shooting of Dan McGrew" that Howie actually laughed, and he was halfway through it before Howie actually leaned back on his haunches, freeing Dwight's arms. Dwight could have socked him in the face – he was mad enough to. But he was scared enough not to. The poetry didn't work as fast as a punch, but the consequences looked more hopeful.

He was exhausted when he finished "The Shooting."

"Can I get up now?" he asked.

"Say it in the duck voice," said Howie cheerfully.

"Can I get up now?" said Dwight in the duck voice.

Howie suddenly leapt up and held out his hand to drag his limp victim to his feet. He even chuckled as he dusted the grass and leaves off him. He quacked himself a few times. "How do you make it come out in words?" he asked.

"It's an old family secret," said Dwight.

"Cool."

Dwight wanted to run now that he was up, but his

limbs all felt like jelly. "Walk me home, you stump-for-brains!" he shouted at Howie in the duck voice. Howie laughed and punched him in the shoulder. Affectionately.

They walked in silence for a few minutes. Gingerly. Dwight was afraid that at any minute, Howie was going to come to his senses. But as they walked along and home got closer and closer, he realized that Howie really didn't have any senses to come to. Dwight had won. Round one, at least.

He waved goodbye to Howie at Howie's place and was moving on up the hill to his own house when Howie called to him. Dwight turned with some trepidation.

"Hey," said Howie. "You should be in Kenny's movie."

Mary Had a Little Lamb

DAVID BOOTH

Mary had a little lamb,
Its fleece was white as snow,
And everywhere that Mary went
– She took it on a bus.

Mary had a little lamb,
Her father shot it dead.
And now it goes to school with her
Between two chunks of bread.

Mary had a little lamb,
It was a greedy glutton.
She fed it ice cream all day long,
And now it's frozen mutton.

Mary had a little lamb,
You've heard this tale before,
But did you know she passed her plate
And had a little more?

Mary had a little cow,
It fed on safety pins.
And every time she milked the cow,
The milk came out in tins.

A Reasonable Sum

GORDON KORMAN

Well, you stayed up all night, but today came anyway. Your head aches, your stomach groans, and your palms are sweaty. In short, you're nervous. You are starting high school today even though you are far too ill to be out of bed.

There is no point in hoping the bus won't show. You can see it in the distance, surer than death and taxes. The yawning doors swallow you up and you pay your fare. On the way to school you make a pact with heaven that you will be good forever – at least, fairly good – in exchange for divine intervention in the horrors to come. Maybe high school can't be avoided, but with help from above, surely some of the blows can be softened.

You arrive at school to find that all those cut-throats who are seven feet tall are your fellow students. The only people who don't have beards are the girls, and even one of them has managed a creditable mustache. You wonder if the school crest depicts a lead pipe on a field of blood red.

Your first assignment is to find your locker, in which will be kept all your worldly possessions. This is far more difficult than it may seem, as all secondary school halls have been laid out as a maze. It's part of a biological experiment designed to discover if high school freshmen are as intelligent as white mice. If you learn to negotiate the halls, you have triumphed over the experiment; if you do not, a shoe box containing your remains will be sent home by third-class mail. It is not a place for the timid or the stupid, and since the most strenuous or intellectually challenging activity of your summer was heating up a TV dinner when the folks were at the country club, you are not in shape for a life-and-death struggle.

Once your locker has been located, you can concern yourself with the intricacies of the combination lock. Since you have a faulty memory for numbers, you have cleverly written your combination, along with all other vital information, on the waistband of your underwear. This system has one serious drawback: it is impossible to maintain your dignity while consulting your notes. Nevertheless, rooting around under your belt in public is infinitely preferable to being found sobbing in front of your unopened locker. 24–26–28. No, that is not your locker combination; that is your underwear size. Finally, the lock opens, and you stow your coat. You are the only one in sight with this particular style of coat. You wonder if, while you were hibernating in front of the television set all summer, fashion changed radically, leaving you a museum piece. Your hair is too short, or maybe a little too long, and – you look down. Your shoes are absurd! Why, there is nothing a peer group sinks its claws into faster than absurd shoes!

Taking a wrong turn on your way to your first class, you are very nearly recruited into a spirited touch football game, but you manage to escape to English class just a little late. The only vacant seat is located right under the teacher's nose, and her hot breath and windmill arm motions begin to take the curl out of your hair. As she rambles on about the joyous learning experiences she has planned for this semester, you muse on something that has been bothering you subconsciously for some time – why is the school office so concerned with obtaining the name, address, and telephone number of your next of kin? Any well-rounded TV addict knows that next of kin are the people notified when the body washes up on the beach. Do they expect you to *die*? Exactly what is the mortality rate in this place?

The teacher then issues a textbook complete with dire warnings of what will happen to you if this book is lost and/or mutilated. She says that you will be charged "a reasonable sum of money" for replacement. The book weighs roughly thirty pounds and has an expensive look about it. You picture yourself washing dishes in the cafeteria for the rest of your life trying to raise the reasonable sum of money.

As you leave the class, it is your misfortune to stumble between two wild-eyed students who are having a ketchup fight. Red slop is flying everywhere. Your first impulse is to save the textbook at all costs. Dropping it to the floor, you fall upon it, shielding its precious pages with your body. Your left shoe is splashed, rendering it even more absurd than before.

Because of a short but perilous trip to the bathroom to clean up, you are late for your next class, which is instrumental music. You rush into the music room, your heart set on a saxophone. They are taken. Your second choice, trumpets, are all in other hands. Ditto, trombones and clarinets. Okay, sacrifice the macho and go for the flute or piccolo. All taken. As a matter of fact, there is only one vacant chair, one instrument at rest. Face it, you are stuck with the tuba.

As you strain to pick it up, you feel your innards drop. You make a mental note to ask your next of kin if your health insurance extends to hernia. The teacher explains how to blow into a tuba. You draw a mighty breath, put your mouth to the mouthpiece (did the guy in period one have pellagra?), and blow until you start to black out. Not a sound. A big cheer goes up from the class as you and the tuba clatter to the floor. The teacher then informs you that, for destruction of an instrument, you will be charged a reasonable sum – in the case of a tuba, about eight hundred dollars. He explains that the instruments may be borrowed for additional practice at home. You have a giddy vision of yourself hauling this brass behemoth onto the bus and being charged another fare for it. Does a tuba qualify for the student discount? Idly, you wonder how your next of kin will take to an evening of oom-pah-pah.

Your French class is right across the hall. Your teacher, who is Madame Something-or-other, hands you a textbook and probably tells you about the reasonable sum. You're not certain, however, because she says it in French. She might have been saying almost anything. Her stream of gibberish virtually uninterrupted, she strolls through the class, stopping directly in front of your desk – the one you had selected as the least noticeable spot in the room. You look up in alarm. Her monologue has ended on a questioning note, and she is looking at you expectantly. You decide to take a stab at it.

"*Oui.*"

She beams, thanks you profusely, and moves on.

A voice comes from behind you. "Psst. Do you know that you just volunteered to make the decorations for our first French party?"

French party? What's a French party? How would you decorate one? When? Where?

You are then exempted from the homework because you have so much to do. As the period ends, you are confronted with a choice. You can stay and find out exactly what is going on, or you can obey your every instinct, which is to run for your life. Retreat wins out. After all, you should get a head start searching for the cafeteria.

You make for your locker but abort that plan to follow an intelligent-looking student who is walking purposefully down the hall carrying a paper bag. In this way you end up in the biology lab where your man rips open the bag, pulls out a dead frog, and begins to dissect it enthusiastically. You stagger out of the lab, no longer hungry.

At length you locate the cafeteria and stare in horror at the chalk board which displays today's menu. Could anyone here know that your mother spearheaded the parents'-group campaign for more nutrition in the school lunches? That your mother, the formerly beloved fairer half of your next of kin, was responsible for today's entree, the alfalfa sloppy joe? You look at all the innocent people in the line behind you and feel a terrible guilt. As you pay the cashier, you notice that there is a big puddle of split-pea soup on the cover of your French book. Oh, no. Is this mutilation? Will you be charged a reasonable sum?

You eat a miserable lunch in the company of a few friends from elementary school. Everything is going along beautifully for them. They are waxing eloquent over the joys of high school, the freedom, the challenge. They don't have to make French decorations. They don't have to play the tuba. They don't already owe a reasonable sum. It's obvious that they are survivors and you are a casualty. What happened to your pact with heaven? Haven't they been paying attention up there? Your friends have obviously been graced with help from above. Why are you the odd man out?

You check the timetable on your underwear and discover to your dismay that your next class is swimming. This is particularly disquieting, since the larger part of your lunch is still lodged in your upper digestive tract. You imagine the coroner's certificate: *Cause of death – sloppy joe.* Well, at least you know where to find the pool.

The water temperature is kept slightly below the tolerance level. This, the instructor informs you, is to keep you active. The only thing that is active, however, is your lunch, which is rising. You know a brief moment of panic as you realize that your clothes are unguarded in the change room. If you lose your underwear, and with it your locker combination and all other vital data, you will never see home again.

"Ten lengths!" As you thrash wretchedly along, fighting off a paralyzing cramp, you wonder if anyone will pull you out if you go under. Probably not. Who would risk hypothermia to save the life of a guy whose mother is a PTA activist responsible for fifteen hundred counts of first degree heartburn? You sincerely hope that, if you die here, your next of kin will charge the school a reasonable sum.

As the class ends, you are just alive enough to listen as the instructor tells you that your crawl is pitiful and that you tread water like a Hovercraft. You would like to explain the extenuating circumstances, but you are hyperventilating.

Soggy but dressed, you move on to your science

class, where you are immediately informed that you are far too wet to work with any electrical equipment. You look around the lab. There is the emergency eyewash and the emergency extinguisher for chemical fires. The radioactive material is kept in that locked cabinet. Everywhere there are signs and instructions on what to do until the doctor comes. This place is obviously a death trap.

A reasonable sum of money will be charged for the loss of an experiment booklet or the destruction of equipment. This is where you learn your first natural law of physics – glass beakers shatter when dropped on the floor. You are standing in the ruins of a whole tray of them. Your socks sparkle with glass slivers, forming regal crowns for your absurd shoes. The debt is mounting.

You decide to stash your books for safety's sake, and find your locker without too much wandering around. You are just about to pat yourself on the back for your powers of navigation when you see it. Someone has scratched an obscene word into the paint of your locker door. It is not just any obscene word, but one of that elite group of obscenities guaranteed to grow hair on the palm of your hand, rarefy the atmosphere, and make a lumberjack blush. Where are you going to find paint to cover up this crime against society before the principal or the morality squad sees it? Everyone knows school lockers are painted in a gray-beige so drab that it can never again be matched. How will you explain your innocence? And why you in the first place? There are rows of lockers in both directions as far as the eye can see, all of them immaculate, and yours is the only one that says ————. This is going to cost you.

You are a good ten minutes late for your last class of the day, Industrial Arts. As you slip into the wood shop and slink toward the nearest vacant seat, the voice of the teacher cuts the air like a razor:

"How considerate of you, young man, to take the time and trouble to appear before us in this humble classroom and gild our wretched selves with your exalted presence. Do sit down and add your genius to our unworthy efforts."

Well, this is the cherry on the bitter ice cream sundae. Heaven, which has seen fit to catapult you from disaster to catastrophe all day, has decided to top your afternoon with the meanest man in the world.

As he lectures on the various pieces of equipment in the shop, with an uncomfortable stress on the damage potential of each, you find it difficult to draw your attention from the razor-sharp stiletto which he is absently using to pare his fingernails. It seems like only yesterday that your teacher marched the class two by two to the local shopping center to visit Santa Claus. Now you are trapped in a wood shop with a maniac with a knife. How time flies.

You are selected for the class demonstration of the wood lathe. The Maniac hands you a partially finished salad bowl, which you fit onto the spindle as per instructions. You flick the switch. The bowl begins to spin, picking up speed. There is an unpleasant screech, and the salad bowl, now a lethal projectile, shoots from the lathe, whistles past the instructor's ear, and sails out the open window into the parking lot. The class breaks into admiring applause.

"You missed me," says the Maniac, following this up with a barrage of abuse and sarcasm aimed directly at you. The class laughs harder with each barb until you sink into your absurd shoes and contemplate a course change. Maybe a history of Teflon manufacturing in Sweden. It might be boring, but at least the teacher won't carry a knife.

As you make your weary way to the bus stop, you notice that the vice-principal's new car has a broken windshield and a salad bowl in the front seat. There is a faint chance that this will be blamed on equipment malfunction and not you, depending on whether the school can charge a reasonable sum for damages occurring outside the building. What if the damage starts inside the building and then leaves, say, by a window? Forget it. Go home. You are ill.

Your next of kin is at the door waiting for you. She asks, "How was your first day at high school, dear?"

A long, elaborate sob story forms in your mind. "Fine," you reply. Next of kin wouldn't understand such things.

I Hate Poetry

LORIS LESYNSKI

I hate poems.
   I hate verse.
      Nothing makes me feel much worse
         than the *rat-ta-tat-tat*
         of the pounding rhyme,
         beat-beat-*beating* on me
            all the time.
   Cat mat hat and
   blink pink ink:
   all should slide down
   the kitchen sink.
Teacher, teacher, what would you say
if I read out loud at *you* all day?
I hate poetry.
I hate rhyme.

That's why I'm ending
without one.

Worn Out

When they're so thin
   you're feeling cold
and elbows poke
   through gaping holes –
when drafts come in
   through big new places
and buttonholes
   are ragged spaces –
when the pictures are faded,
   the bottom's in shreds,
and most of the top is just
   hanging in threads,
look at yourself
   by the light of the moon:
   you need new pajamas.

Soon.

from

Never Sleep Three in a Bed

MAX BRAITHWAITE

And that brings me to Charles Dickens and Goofy Hendrickson and the Cratchits' Christmas dinner. I don't know how a kid picks up a nickname like "Goofy." The same way I got tagged "Fat," I guess, and Eugene Ellingson became known as "Puss," and Ernie Roberts became known as "Pants." A whole book could be written about how kids get their nicknames, and why. Anyway, Goofy Hendrickson had picked up the tag, and it stayed with him. He was the only kid we knew who ate crayons, and he had this interesting habit of tattooing himself with his straight pen by running the nib under the skin of the back of his hands and arms. He also swore a lot. His dad worked for Burns and Co. in their stockyard, and swearing was a necessary accessory to his job. Goofy picked up some expressions that even *we* hadn't heard, and frequently used to beguile us with them.

We were in Grade Seven by now. The teacher was Miss Bishop, and she was pretty and I was in love with her. But not the way I was in love with Elva Mawhinney who sat across the aisle from me. Elva was petite and dark-haired, and had the prettiest little mouth you ever saw. Everything about her was pretty. The way she leaned her chin on her fist when she read from the reader. The way she rested her plump pink arm on the desk when she wrote. The way she tossed her dark curls when she turned her head. The way she walked. The way she did everything just sent me up the wall.

Dickens' *A Christmas Carol* was our supplementary reading and, as every teacher since the story was written has surely done, Miss Bishop decided that we would dramatize the Cratchits' Christmas dinner for the school's Christmas concert. Fine. I was chosen as Bob Cratchit, I suppose because he was tall and skinny and I was short and stout. I sure did hope that Elva Mawhinney would be chosen as Martha, because there's one part in the story where she runs into Bob's arms and he kisses her. Yeeow!

But things never work out perfectly in this imperfect world. Elva was chosen to be one of the young Cratchits – you know, the ones that were steeped in sage and onions to their eyebrows. Goofy Hendrickson was the other one, I suppose because he was the tallest kid in the room and looked about as much like a young Cratchit as he did like a jack-rabbit.

The part of Martha? That went to Edna Trumper. What can I say about Edna? She wasn't petite and frilly like Elva, that's certain. She was kind of long and skinny. And she wore a coarse cotton dress, and coarse cotton stockings and boots. She was a fine girl, though, and certainly did fit the part of Martha, but I could never figure why Miss Bishop – in just this one instance – should suddenly resort to perfect type-casting.

Well, you know the Dickens story. It's full of bounce and good spirits, and is everybody's idea of Christmas dinner. Let's face it, Christmas as we know it was invented by Charles Dickens. But our performance somehow lacked some of the necessary verve and enthusiasm. We wandered about the front of the room mumbling our lines and, try as she would, Miss Bishop couldn't inject any life into the performance – especially into that kissing scene.

Let me see – the exact words from the story are, "she came prematurely from behind the closet door and ran into his arms." It doesn't say anything about Bob Cratchit running the other way, or keeping his arms at his sides, or turning his head and blushing red as a sunset, or trying to dodge. None of that is there at all.

"Come now, Max," Miss Bishop would urge. "You can do better than that. Don't be shy."

How could I explain to her that if she'd just put Elva Mawhinney in that part, she wouldn't need to worry about my shyness. She'd have trouble the other way round, I'll be bound. But I couldn't say that, so I rather welcomed the shyness-bit.

Oddly enough, the only one who showed any real feeling for his part was Goofy Hendrickson. He really dug it. Ran around shouting about sage and onions and pinching the other young Cratchit – Elva – and pulling her hair, and making her dimple all over the place. And when they squeezed into the corner together, as the script called for, it seemed to me he squeezed too damned hard.

Then came the actual eating scene. Here, although he has described a Christmas dinner better than anyone else ever could, Dickens thoughtlessly didn't write down any actual dialogue for his characters to speak. Miss Bishop, being no playwright, had not assayed to correct that deficiency.

"Just talk the way you would normally," she advised, not realizing what she was saying. And we did pretty well at it in rehearsals. I said "There never was such a goose cooked," and Mrs. Cratchit cried with great delight, "We haven't eaten it all at last!" and the young Cratchits filled in the script with "yum yums," and such a deal of smacking of lips as to make even Scrooge blush.

But came opening night. Or opening afternoon, I should say, and something happened to us thespians. As soon as we saw parents and others coming into that school auditorium, we got buck-fever and got it bad. As a result, we all got sort of hopped up and overdid everything. If we were supposed to speak out, we shouted. If we were supposed to walk fast, we rushed. So when I came in through the curtain as Bob Cratchit, and said my bit about "Where's Martha?" and she came to the part where it says, "ran into his arms," she came out of the cupboard like a lioness coming at a zebra. Naturally I took a backward step, tripped over a stool and fell flat on my back.

The whole thing rather fell apart after that. Nobody could seem to remember what to say or where to stand, with the result that we walked over each others' lines, and into each others' persons, and the play was a shambles. There was a rustle in the wings, which I was sure must be Charles Dickens turning over in his grave, but actually was Miss Bishop, trying to whisper directions to us.

The grand dénouement of all this confusion came with the dinner table scene when the goose was brought in. Nobody could think of a single bright *ad lib*, and we all sat there, heads down, utensils moving foolishly as we stuffed forkfuls of nothing into our tongue-tied mouths. From the wings Miss Bishop kept urging, "Say something, say something, say *something*!"

And finally she got through at least to Goofy. His frightened, benumbed brain finally grasped the idea. A big, stupid smile spread across his homely face. He carefully laid down his knife and fork, turned full face to the audience, and yelled: "It's the best sonofabitch goose ever I et!"

Introducing Norbert

RICHARD SCRIMGER

It sounds like an easy topic for a science report. The Moons of Jupiter. Lots of books on Jupiter in the library, lots of stuff on CD-ROM. Pictures, articles. Might even be interesting. But I'm having just a heck of a time writing it, because Norbert is very sensitive on the topic.

– *I am not sensitive*, says Norbert.

"Yes you are," I tell him. "You're very sensitive. All I have to do is mention the word Jupiter and you start to twitch."

– *That's because I know so much about it. After all, it's where I come from*, he says.

I'd better introduce myself. I'm Alan. I live in a small town in Ontario. Actually my notebook reads Cobourg Ontario Canada North America The World. I'm thirteen years old and in Grade Seven. I have brown hair and brown eyes and a big mouth, at least that's what my friend Victor tells me. And just above my mouth, in the regular place, I have a nose. Not a regular sort of nose though. Oh, it looks normal enough – couple of freckles, occasional smudge of dirt. It drips when I have a cold, and wrinkles up when I'm thinking hard, or when there's cabbage for dinner, but . . . well . . . I don't know how to put it, except to say I'm trying to do some research for this science project only my nose won't let me. His name is Norbert.

– *Do I say hello now?*

"If you like," I say.

– *Hello. My name is Norbert Nose. I'm from the biggest planet. And the nicest.*

Norbert is talking about Jupiter. He usually ends up talking about Jupiter. And he says the craziest things.

– *Craziest?*

"Oops. Sorry, Norbert," I say. I forgot he was reading this.

– *What kind of crazy things?*

"Well, you said that Jupiter is full of noses."

– *It is.*

"The noses have little feet apparently, and no arms.

And they hop everywhere. They have telephones and spaceships and all sorts of technology, but all they want to do is hop. And when they get tired of hopping, they put up their feet and take a nap. I'm sorry, Norbert, but it really does sound crazy to me."

Norbert gives a little satirical laugh: it sounds like this – *heu heu. You should know about crazy*, he says, *you're the one talking to his own nose!*

He may have a point there.

I found out about my nose about a year ago, when he sneezed (that's what I think now; at the time I thought I was the one sneezing) and then said – *Bless me.* In a little tiny voice. Norbert isn't very old, three or four years, but as he's constantly reminding me, a year on Jupiter is really four or five of ours, so Norbert is really almost twenty years old. Quite old, to be drinking cocoa and taking afternoon naps.

– *I like cocoa. On Jupiter everyone drinks cocoa. It's our national drink.*

Can you guess what I asked him first? No, nothing about colds, or sunburns or what it feels like to have a fingernail poking in your living room. I asked him what had happened to my own nose. I mean my real nose, the one I had until he came along.

– *Your nose is still there. That's why you look the same as before. And I'm here too. It's a big place, your nose. There's a back room, and a kitchen and bathroom, and a garage.*

I still have trouble understanding this. But my nose wrinkles up the way it used to, and feels itchy in the summer. It's still my nose – but it's Norbert too. I don't know how to explain it, and neither does Norbert.

"What's in the garage?" I had to ask.

– *A spaceship, you fish!* Norbert can be quite arrogant. He thinks a fish is the ultimate insult – maybe because fish don't have noses. I must remember to show him a picture of a swordfish one of these days. *How else do you think I got here from Jupiter?*

I asked him about other people. Do their noses come from Jupiter too? He snorted, unless it was a sigh. – *No no, I'm kind of a gypsy. Most noses are happy on Jupiter, but ever since I lost Nerissa I've wanted to travel.*

"Oh," I said, kind of serious, because he seemed so sad. He sniffed a bit – usually he hates sniffing. I wondered about his story. An unhappy love affair, it sounded like. Forget Nerissa, I wanted to tell him. No nose is worth it. What is she? – a rag and a cartilage and a hank of hair. But I never did tell him.

Let's get back to the project. I'm in the library now, staring at the cover of a book about Jupiter. I've been staring at it for a while.

– *A beautiful picture*, Norbert comments. *I think I can see the street where I used to live.*

"Come on, Norbert. The project is due tomorrow." I open the book to the chapter on Jupiter's moons and start reading. Pretty soon Norbert is twitching and making funny noises. "What is it?" I whisper.

– *Wrong*, he says. *All wrong. Wrong wrong wrong.*

I ask what's all wrong.

– *Everything. The part you have your finger on right now.*

"Where it says there are at least thirteen moons?" I whisper. "What's wrong with that?"

– *There are only three moons.*

"Norbert," I say, "this is a picture from the Voyager spaceship. There are lots of moons circling Jupiter."

– *Three. I know.*

"Then what are the other moons all doing in the picture?" I ask.

– *They're there for a birthday party.*

"That's ridiculous."

– *There are pictures from your last birthday party, Alan. A dozen kids, waving at the camera and holding balloons. Are they all in your family?*

"Wait a minute. You're saying that if Voyager had taken the pictures later on, there'd have been only three moons?"

– *That's right. Ganymede, Hyperion, and Sid.*

"One of the moons on Jupiter is named Sid? I can't believe it."

– *That's what we call him. In Jupiter's legends Sid is known as the Bringer of Cocoa.*

"Norbert, I cannot report to my class that one of Jupiter's moons is called Sid. Remember, we have to read these projects out loud. Can you imagine what Ms Scathely would say."

– *What if I read that part?* he says.

"No," I say firmly. "Remember the bath."

Norbert has a charming voice (I have to be nice because he's reading this) but it's a little bit high and squeaky. I was taking a bath and my mom came right up to the door and asked if everything was all right. "I heard two voices," she said. I don't know what she thought was going on. I told her I was fine, and then Norbert said that actually he preferred showers. *Everyone on Jupiter takes showers,* he said. There was this long silence from outside and then mom said, "Oh." She didn't come in, but I heard her muttering to herself about puberty.

"Oh, hi, Alan," I look up from my book. It's Miranda. She's in my class at school.

"Hi," I say. I must be more worried than I thought because I didn't notice her coming over to talk to me. I usually notice Miranda. She has these great big eyes and a really pretty smile. She's taller than I am, and she can run faster and jump higher and hit a baseball farther than I can. And she's smarter. Good thing she's only a girl or I'd have a real inferiority complex.

Actually, I kind of like her. But I didn't think she even knew I was around.

"Still working on your project?" she asks.

"Huh?"

"Jupiter." She points to the book in my hand.

The librarian frowns over at us. You wonder if maybe they were born with that expression on their faces. I've never seen them look any other way.

"Oh." I smile at Miranda. "Right." Silver tongue, that's me. I remind myself of those teenage guys on afternoon TV. "How about you? You're finished your project, I bet." I'm smiling so hard my face hurts.

"Yes. Last week." She turns away, touches the tip of her nose. Her eyes are closed. She looks like she's going to sneeze. "Excuse me." She sneezes.

– Bless you, says Norbert.

"Shut up," I tell him in a furious whisper.

"What was that, Alan?"

"Nothing." She stares at me. I can feel myself getting red.

"Young man." It's the librarian. Who else calls you

"young man"? She points to her lips. "I must ask you to be quiet."

I don't know how long I sit there reading the book. Not very long. I try to pay attention to what I'm reading but Norbert won't let me. He starts fizzing and spitting and getting all worked up. The librarian tells me to be quiet again. I tell her I'm sorry, and whisper at Norbert to be quiet. People are staring at me from behind their books. I now know how a mom feels when her baby is acting up. I lose my temper and threaten Norbert with a Kleenex – but nothing works. He starts shouting.

I'm reading about the poisonous atmosphere of Jupiter and its moons, and Norbert is screaming at the top of his voice, telling me what a great atmosphere it was, that noses come from all over Jupiter to breathe in the atmosphere of the moons. That's when the librarian kicks me out. She says she's sorry but she isn't, not really.

Miranda is waiting for me at the door. "Alan, I'd like to talk to you," she says.

Ordinarily I'd have fallen over myself at this point, but I'm really upset. Also, I'm mad at Norbert. "I'll see you at school," I say, brushing past her and jumping on my bike.

Ever had an argument with your nose? Don't try it, you'll lose. I yell at Norbert and he drips on me. I pinch him and he sneezes, explodes all over me. Yuck. I give up. "All right, Norbert," I say, finally. "You win. Just answer me this. What am I going to do now? I have to hand in the project tomorrow. I'll have to write it all tonight. I'll have to stay up late, and I'm already tired. And I have no idea what I'm going to say. There's no data at home on Jupiter, no encyclopedias or *National Geographics*. We have an old computer – no internet, no CD-ROM. And they won't let me back in the library. What am I going to do? You got me into this mess – now get me out of it!"

– *All right*, he says, *I will*.

"Did you finish your project?" Mom asks me at dinner time. Liver and cabbage. Not my favorite, but I know Norbert likes it. Nice and smelly. I hope he's happy.

"No," I say. "I'll have to work some more on it after dinner."

I yawn. Her face softens. She knows it's due tomorrow. She knows I'm tired. "Is there anything I can do to help?" she asks.

I smile at her. She means well but she has no idea. "You could get me a cup of cocoa," I say.

"I didn't know you liked cocoa, Alan."

"Just trying to get in a Jupiter frame of mind," I tell her.

Norbert is so confident. – *Don't worry*, he says. *I know more about Jupiter than any encyclopedia. Your space probe took pictures of the moons, but I was there.*

"You were?" I must be crazy, I'm believing him here.

– *Of course. Just sit back and type what I tell you.* He sounds like he really does know what he's talking about. I relax a little bit. I turn on the computer, take a sip of cocoa and flex my typing fingers – both of them.

"Ready when you are," I say.

He clears his throat – that sounds silly, a nose clearing its throat, but that's what it sounds like – *Hmm hmm. Ganymede, the largest of Jupiter's satellites, is a forbidding place*, he says. That sounds pretty good. I start to type. He keeps talking and I keep typing. At the back of my mind I'm a little worried about what's going to happen when we get to Sid, but I'll go along for now. It doesn't sound bad. – *High basalt cliffs and barren dusty plains are sterile and lifeless . . .* I type away. I'm yawning like crazy, I make a couple of mistakes, blink a bit. I hear Norbert's voice as a kind of sing-song. – *Lullaby, and good night*. I sit up straight. Did he say that, or did I dream it? Mom comes in to wish me good night and good luck. Back to the keyboard. I concentrate on my typing. Norbert drones on. I'm paying more attention to my two fingers than to my ears, typing without listening. I shake my head and blink. Sleepy. So sleepy . . .

I wake up with my face on the keyboard. Two in the morning. I've been asleep. I'm tired, and I have to go to the bathroom. I look up at the screen – and I can't believe my eyes. Somehow the project is done. I've printed up ten pages and the words at the bottom of the last page are THE END. Wow. I yawn.

My nose hurts. Last time it felt like that was a couple of years ago when I walked into a glass door. Poor Norbert has been wearing himself out, working so hard. He must be sleeping now, with his feet up in the back room. I wash my face in cold water, and he wakes up briefly. "Thanks," I tell him.

– *Ouch*.

If Mom hadn't knocked on my door next morning I'd probably still be sleeping. "School bus in ten minutes," she says.

I almost forget the project in my rush to get ready. Norbert reminds me. There's just time to staple the sheets together and cram them into my knapsack.

"Did you get it done, Alan?" asks Victor, as we're bouncing over the railway tracks.

"Oh sure," I say. "No problem." What a liar I am.

"I tell you, I am not looking forward to reading mine out loud," says Victor. "My project is so . . . *boring*. Everyone is going to fall asleep."

No one falls asleep during my reading.

No one looks bored. No one coughs or fidgets. For the first minute or so, the only sound apart from my voice is a collective intake of breath.

And then the whole class starts to laugh.

Ms Scathely leads the way with a restrained little tee-hee, hand over her face, then a couple of girls in the front row snicker to each other. When I get to the part about the beaches on Hyperion, with fountains of cocoa and bright warm sun every day except Thursday, when Ganymede gets in the way, Ms Scathely's shoulders are shaking. She's trying to control herself but she can't, she's laughing too hard, and she slips right off her chair and falls to the floor going, "Whoop . . . whoop . . . whoop." The class erupts like a one-room volcano, shouts of laughter, pencils and notebooks flying in the air. I stop reading at about this time, because no one can hear me. I'm about done anyway. My face is red and glowing, like lava, I guess. Appropriate. I'm not embarrassed though – well, I am of course, but that's not all I am. I'm mad. Ms Scathely is on the floor, sobbing with mirth, my friends are shouting and carrying on, and I'm wondering how I go about punching myself in the nose. Wait until I get Norbert alone: I'll blow his ears off, I'll put a clothespin on him, I'll smoke a pack of cigarettes, I'll stick an entire box of Kleenex – yes, it is pretty funny, I suppose, but I'm not in the mood.

If only I'd stayed awake. If only I'd checked the project last night, or this morning.

– *What's a clothespin?*

"Never mind." I keep forgetting Norbert can read.

– *You aren't really angry, are you, Alan? Not now that it's all turned out so well. If it weren't for me writing your project, think what you'd have missed!*

"You too," I say.

– *Yes. Me too.*

"How did it go today?" Mom asks.

I'm not mad any more. If you want to know, I'm bursting with excitement and happiness inside, but I don't tell Mom. I'm casual. "Got an A +," I say. Like this happens all the time.

"ALAN!"

"Ms Scathely said it was the most . . . original piece of work she'd ever heard." She also said it was the goofiest, but I didn't pass that on. "She wants me to send it to a magazine. Maybe it'll be published."

"Oh Alan, I'm so proud of you!"

I perch myself on the counter, push back my hair. "What's for dinner?"

"What would you like?"

"Spaghetti," I say. "And," very cool now, "I'd like to . . . um . . . invite someone over."

"Miranda?"

How do moms do that? I haven't talked about her more than a couple of times. I close my mouth, nod. "She's asking her parents. She doesn't think there'll be a problem."

Miranda came up to me in the hallway after class, her eyes shining. I was still mad and embarrassed. The rest of the class were on their way to history, still laughing. The bell rang. "I knew it, Alan," she said. "I knew it yesterday in the library."

"Huh?" I may have mentioned how suave I get around Miranda. "Knew what?"

"Knew you were like me." She put her hands on my shoulders. "That stuff about Jupiter. I know about it too. I was too scared to put it in my project, but you weren't."

"Huh?"

"Oh, Alan, I know. I know where your database is." She arched her eyebrows and gave a squiggly smile. Modern flirting. When they're interested in your database, you've got them.

"Oh yeah?" I say.

"Yeah." And right there in the empty hallway, we were both going to be late for our history class, she leaned down and, well, we rubbed noses.

– *Hey!* Norbert must have been napping. I'd forgotten about him.

Miranda giggled. And this teeny weeny little voice shrieked out – *Norbert! Norbert, is it you? Oh Norbert I've missed you so.*

Another nose from Jupiter.

– *Nerissa! I've missed you too.*

We walked down the hall, the four of us, talking all the time. The late bell rang. Nerissa and Norbert exchanged telephone numbers. Miranda and I ran to class.

The Sitter and the Butter and the Better Batter Fritter

DENNIS LEE

My little sister's sitter
Got a cutter from the baker,
And she baked a little fritter
From a pat of bitter butter.
First she bought a butter beater
Just to beat the butter better,
And she beat the bit of butter
   With the beater that she bought.

Then she cut the bit of butter
With the little butter cutter,
And she baked the beaten butter
In a beaten butter baker.
But the butter was too bitter
And she couldn't eat the fritter

So she set it by the cutter
　And the beater that she bought.

And I guess it must have taught her
Not to use such bitter butter,
For she bought a bit of batter
That was sweeter than the butter.
And she cut the sweeter batter
With the cutter, and she beat her
Sweeter batter with a sweeter batter
　Beater that she bought.

Then she baked a batter fritter
That was better than the butter
And she ate the better batter fritter
　Just like that.

But while the better batter
Fritter sat inside the sitter –
Why, the little bitter fritter
Made of bitter butter bit her,
Bit my little sister's sitter
　Till she simply disappeared.

Then my sister came to meet her
But she couldn't see the sitter –
She just saw the bitter butter

Fritter that had gone and et her;
So she ate the butter fritter
   With a teaspoonful of jam.

Now my sister has a bitter
Butter fritter sitting in her,
And a sitter in the bitter
Butter fritter, since it ate her,
And a better batter fritter
Sitting in the silly sitter
In the bitter butter fritter
   Sitting in my sister's tum.

The Day of the Raisin

MARTYN GODFREY

This is a true story. Everything in it actually happened in my school. I am honestly not making this up.

Before becoming a full-time writer, I used to teach elementary and junior-high school. I taught for eleven years. That's well over two thousand days inside the classroom. I have to admit those days have blurred in my memory.

Except one.

The memory of one day is so sharp; it's as if I have a videotape playing in my head. It was the day of the raisin.

Our school didn't have a lunchroom or a cafeteria, so the students who stayed for lunch ate in their classroom. As soon as the lunch buzzer rang on the day of the raisin, several of my eighth-grade girls shoved some desks together so they could talk to each other while they ate. Watching them was Kevin, the boy who wore the title of Class Clown with pride.

Kevin regarded the clump of girls and a devilish grin creased his face. "I'm going to go over to the girls," he thought. "And I'm going to gross them out."

He opened his lunch bag and discovered his mom had thrown in a sandwich, a juice box, and one of those tiny packets of raisins. When no one was looking, he removed a single raisin and pushed it up his left nostril.

I repeat, I am honestly not making this up.

You may think his plan was to walk over to the girls, squeeze his right nostril shut, blow the raisin out of his left nostril, and start laughing. Nope, Kevin was more creative than that.

We'd had a math assignment that morning, a worksheet with word problems. Kevin took his copy of the worksheet over to the girls and asked for their help in solving the questions. His plan was to wait a few minutes, until the girls were halfway through their sandwiches, stop discussing the math assignment, twitch his nose, and say, "Hey, my nose feels weird. It's never felt like this before. I wonder . . . would you excuse me for a moment while I check out my nose?" Then he planned to put his finger up his left nostril, pick his nose ever so slowly, pull the raisin out, wave it in front of the girls, and proudly pro-claim, "Hey, check out the size of this sucker!"

Of course, the girls would be utterly and com-pletely grossed out.

Unfortunately, the plan didn't work out as planned.

What went wrong? Well, when I was talking to the doctor after school, she told me raisins are dried-up grapes and the inside of your nose is a fairly moist place. The doc reasoned that, since Kevin had the raisin in his nose for several minutes, it may have soft-ened up a little.

Maybe. But I think what really went wrong was the raisin was just *too big* in the first place. You see, when Kevin got to the "My nose feels weird" part of his plan and inserted his finger into his nostril, he discov-ered there was no room to get his finger beside the raisin to flick it out. In his effort to get the raisin, he shoved it further and further into his nose.

Of course, Kevin succeeded in grossing out those poor girls. They didn't have a clue what he was doing. Can you imagine eating your lunch and suddenly there's someone standing over you with a finger shoved way up his nose, digging around for some-thing? We'd all be grossed out.

We later found out from Kevin that, at this point, he went to the boys' bathroom and tried to blow the raisin out.

No luck.

The doctor explained to me why he couldn't remove it from his nose and, although I'm tempted to give you the gory details, I think I'd better just say, "It was stuck."

Stuck real good.

So now Kevin was faced with a dilemma. He's in the eighth grade. Not kindergarten. He's thirteen years old. Not three years old. What should he do?

Tell his friends? "Hey, guys, you'll never guess what just happened in my nose."

No. Bad move.

Go to the office? "Excuse me, sir, I have a slight problem inside my nose."

No. Certainly not.

Phone home? "Hey, Mom, you remember those raisins you put in my lunch? One of them got stuck in my nose. Weird, huh?"

Not a chance.

Tell his homeroom teacher? "Yo, Mr. Godfrey, you'll never guess what's in my nose."

Nix to that idea too.

So Kevin did absolutely nothing. He spent the next thirty minutes of lunch with a raisin stuck up his nose. Think about that. It definitely wasn't a pleasant experience.

We were fifteen minutes into Language Arts class

before I noticed something was wrong with Kevin. He still hadn't told anyone his problem, but I knew he was in trouble. Kevin was sitting in his desk, the front seat of the outside row, with his hand resting on the left side of his face and, more unusual, he was breathing through his mouth.

"Kevin," I said. "What's up? Do you have a headache?"

He shook his head sheepishly. "No."

"Do you have something in your eye?" I wondered.

Another gentle shake of his head. "No."

Now my curiosity was fired. "Kevin, what the heck are you doing?"

He beckoned me with his right hand. I walked over to his desk, bent over because Kevin was whispering, and heard the strangest sentence of my teaching career. "Mr. Godfrey, I have a raisin in my nose."

I stared at him in shocked silence. Had I heard correctly?

Kevin whispered because he didn't want anyone else in the class to hear what he was saying. He wanted only me to know. Unfortunately, Shannon, the girl who sat next to him, heard the whisper or read his lips. She glanced at me and in a loud, surprised voice exclaimed. "He says he's got a raisin in his nose."

My eighth-grade class immediately woke up.

If a thirteen-year-old boy told you he had a raisin in his nose, your first reaction would probably be, "Right, tell me another." That was my reaction. I didn't believe Kevin. I thought he was joking.

"What do you mean?" I puzzled. "You have a raisin in your nose? How did you get a raisin in your nose?"

"I put it there," he answered.

"You *put* it there?" I mumbled in disbelief. "Kevin, why would you put a raisin up your nose?"

Before Kevin had time to answer, one of the boys at the back of the class yelled, "He's saving it for later."

Of course, that broke the class up.

Kevin got a little weepy. I could tell it was taking everything he had to hold back the tears. So I took him to the office and knocked on the principal's door.

I wish I'd had a camera. The scene in the office would have won the photo-of-the-year award. There was Kevin, sitting in a chair, explaining the facts of his misadventure to the principal, Mr. Nightingale. I'm sure every principal in the country has heard a truckload of unusual stories from their students, but I could tell by the amazement etched into his face this was the weirdest tale Mr. Nightingale had ever encountered. All the principal could mutter was. "No kidding? No kidding?"

When Kevin finished (this is the point when I wanted a camera; this was the Kodak Moment), the principal said, "Let me see." Mr. Nightingale actually peered up Kevin's nose. I couldn't help but laugh.

We took Kevin to the local clinic where the doctor removed the raisin with an instrument Kevin described as "a long, skinny, hooked pair of tweezers." As soon as the raisin was out, Kevin asked the doc, "Is it okay if I keep the raisin?"

I repeat for a second time, I am *honestly* not making this up.

Well, the silly doctor dropped the raisin into a plastic pill vial and handed it to Kevin. Which he brought back to school.

When Kevin walked into the classroom, there was an immediate buzz from everyone. I hadn't told my students the particulars of Kevin's misfortune. We all know junior-highs can be merciless with their teasing and I wanted to protect Kevin. I didn't have to be concerned. Kevin stood proudly at the front of the classroom, pulled the pill vial from his pocket and held it above his head. "A half-hour ago," he proclaimed, "this baby was stuck in my nose."

"Wow!" several students yelled.

"Awesome!" a few others called out.

Someone said, "Cool."

"Gross me out!" Shannon complained.

You can see why I have such a good memory of the day. It is something I'll never forget.

For the rest of the year, Kevin was definitely a celebrity in the school. People started calling him the Raisin Man, a nickname Kevin enjoyed.

Several weeks later, Kevin's Home Ec assignment was to bake cookies. He made raisin cookies. When he offered one to me, I took it and said, "I'll eat it later." I confess that I never did eat the cookie. I just couldn't. I mean, you never know where those raisins have been.

Baseball Riddles

Question: A man was running home. A masked man jumped out at him. Then the man ran back to where he came from. Where did he come from?
Answer: Third base.
(Jacqui McIsaac, Notre Dame School, Newmarket, Ontario)

Question: What baseball player holds the most liquid?
Answer: The pitcher.
(Kathryn Psutka, Blessed Kateri Tekakwitha School, North York, Ontario)

Tales from the Negro Leagues

LORNE BROWN

In the Negro Leagues the owners were black, the managers were black, the players were black, the fans were black.

Only the ball was white.

Did you ever hear of a fellow called Cool Papa Bell? Now Cool Papa Bell was a great ballplayer. He was fast. Now when I say he was fast, what I mean to imply is that he was fast. Cool Papa Bell once was standing in the batter's box. The pitcher threw the ball and Bell hit a line drive right back through the pitcher's box and Cool Papa Bell was called out at second base by the umpire for being hit by his own batted ball. Now that's fast!

Now in those days the rookies roomed with the veteran players, and of course there was not much money, so the hotel room would not be a great hotel room. Now when Cool Papa Bell was a rookie, he and this veteran were getting into bed in the middle of an old room with no other furniture. There was only one light, in the middle of the ceiling, hanging down from a long cord. The light switch was by the door. The veteran told Cool Papa Bell to turn the light out. Now Cool Papa Bell was fast. He was so fast he turned out the light switch and was back in bed before the light turned off! He was fast.

There was a pitcher then called Satchel Paige. Some of you may have heard of old Satch? Yep . . . Old Satch was fast, too. When he threw the ball, it was fast. He, himself, was rather slow, but he could throw that ball fast.

He could throw so fast that when he threw the ball through a rainstorm the ball wouldn't even get wet. He could throw it so fast that sometimes he would stand up there, act like he was going to throw the ball. The catcher would pound his mitt as if he had caught the ball and the umpire would call "*Strike!*" And the batter would say, "Jeeze Old Satch is fast today – I never even saw that pitch."

They used to call him "The Barber." He'd throw a ball so hard close to the batter's face that he shaved the beard off his face when the ball went by. That's why they called him "The Barber."

Old Satch was a bit of a philosopher, too, and when someone asked him the secret of his success, he said, "Don't look back; something might be gaining on you."

Old Satch used to advertise himself as "The World's Greatest Pitcher – guaranteed to strike out the first nine men." After he struck out the first nine batters he often would deliberately load the bases. Bases on balls to three batters in a row. Bases loaded. Nobody out. Then Old Satch, he'd turn around, wave the outfielders to come sit in the dugout. When the outfield was sitting in the dugout, he'd proceed to strike out the next three batters in a row!

Remember I told you about the catcher pounding his mitt when Satchel Paige was throwing the ball? That catcher's name was Josh Gibson. Josh Gibson could hit the ball. Let me tell you, he could hit the ball! He could hit the ball! He could hit that ball so hard that people called him the Black Babe Ruth. But people who really knew their baseball called Babe Ruth the white Josh Gibson!

Josh Gibson hit the ball out of Yankee Stadium. Now nobody else has ever hit the ball out of Yankee Stadium. Babe Ruth never did that. Mickey Mantle never did that. Reggie Jackson never did that. Josh

Gibson did that. Two hundred thousand people saw Josh Gibson hit the ball out of Yankee Stadium. Of course in those days, Yankee Stadium only held sixty thousand people but there have been at least two hundred thousand people say, "I was there the day Josh Gibson hit the ball out of Yankee Stadium!"

He played for a team called the Pittsburgh Grays. One time Pittsburgh and Philly were having a home and home series – the first game in Pittsburgh and the second one in Philadelphia. Now the games were played in those days in the afternoon. They didn't have any lights in the ball park. Now the game was tied, and it went on and on, and it got darker and darker. Finally Philadelphia went ahead 2–0. In the bottom of the inning, the home half of the inning, Pittsburgh loaded the bases. There were two out and Josh Gibson came to the plate.

It was getting dark.

The pitcher wound up and he threw the ball. Josh Gibson hit the ball. Oh did he hit that ball. Godawmighty, did he hit that ball! It went up into the sky. It was getting dark. That ball went up.

It didn't come down!

It got really dark.

The umpires looked at each other . . .

Well, they had to call it a home run. What else could they do? So Pittsburgh won the game.

Now I told you this was a home and home series. Next afternoon they were at Philadelphia. This was a bright sunny afternoon – you don't have to worry about the game being called on account of darkness. Well, it's in Philadelphia, so Philadelphia takes to the field. Pittsburgh Grays, they're gonna go to bat. They got their batter in the batter's box, there. Suddenly the crowd started saying, "Look at the center fielder!"

Everybody looks at the center fielder – this guy must be crazy – he's running around in circles, looking up at the sky. Everybody looks up at the sky – there's a little dot up there – little dot gets bigger. The center fielder is running around in circles, but ever narrower circles. He gets himself right under that thing that's coming down. It's a ball! It's coming down and he catches it. The force of it knocks him right over but he manages to hold onto the ball.

The umpire, quick as a wink calls, "Josh Gibson, you're out yesterday in Pittsburgh – Philadelphia wins the game!"

Gross

KEN ROBERTS

Albert lived in Whitby, Ontario, on the north shore of Lake Ontario just east of Toronto. He was the youngest of seven children, and he liked to talk. Everyone in his family liked to talk. Unfortunately, Albert also liked people to listen.

Dinnertime was the best time to talk in Albert's family. His parents insisted that everyone sit at the table and eat together. Nobody could watch television, except on Sundays when Albert's parents ordered a pizza and rented a movie. Dinner was a time to talk, which was fine with Albert's three older brothers and three older sisters, two of whom were twins.

When Albert was old enough to say a few words at the dinner table (which he did at an early age because he was exposed to so much talking), most of his brothers and sisters and both his parents stopped their conversations and listened and laughed and patted Albert on the head. This, of course, made Albert talk more, but the family, busy with their own conversations, stopped listening.

By the time Albert was six years old, he was desperate. Nobody ever listened.

Albert tried talking about dinosaurs and pirates and cartoon characters and games he'd learned at school, but nobody seemed interested at all. He tried creating an imaginary girlfriend, since girlfriends seemed a topic which his brothers and sisters enjoyed, but all that happened was one sister snorted and his Dad laughed. No more.

Then, one magical evening, or so Albert thought at the time, he said, "They gave us shots at school today" during a semi-break in the dinnertime conversation.

"Oh yeah?" said one of his brothers. "Did you look away or did you watch the needle go into your arm?"

"I watched," said Albert, even though he hadn't and the thought of actually watching made him feel a little bit sick.

"Awwgh," said one of Albert's other older brothers. "I never watch. It's too gross."

And then Albert's six brothers and sisters, and his parents too, all talked about whether they watched when they got shots and whether or not they could watch scenes on television when actors got shots and whether famous actors actually had to get the shots themselves or if they used stunt doubles for the close-up pictures of their arms when the needles were inserted.

Nobody paid much attention to Albert, but he didn't care. Albert was listening, closely, because he knew that something he'd said had interested every-one at the table.

Albert ate quietly. And he ate quietly for the next few nights, too, listening instead of trying to talk, figuring out what might attract attention when he finally did say something again.

Eight nights later, during a small break in the din-nertime babble, Albert opened his mouth and, using his high-pitched voice, told his entire family that "Marty from Grade Three brought a cheese sandwich to school today but after he'd eaten half of it he noticed that the cheese was green with mold."

"Awgh!" said the twin sisters together.

"Awgh!" said Albert's father a moment later.

"Eat your greens," said Albert's mom.

"Mom!" shouted the sister who wasn't a twin.

Albert's mom frowned for a second and then realized that she'd said the word green and green was the color of the mold in Marty's sandwich. "Sorry," she said.

KEN ROBERTS

Albert smiled.

"Marty ate the sandwich anyway," he added.

"Gross," said Albert's father.

Over the next few months, Albert managed to talk about pus and scabs and nose drips and various forms of rotting food and pimples and warts and hairs which grew in pairs from tiny little bumps on his father's neck.

Albert was careful not to discuss anything to do with fighting or guns since his parents would not tolerate discussions about violence at any time, particularly dinnertime.

By the time he was eight years old, the only things Albert ever talked about at the dinner table were topics which could be considered stomach-churningly gross.

Albert could discuss infectious diseases, famous disasters, exploding belly buttons, and the fact that alligators drag their victims to the bottom of swamps and tuck them under logs to ripen.

Albert's parents didn't seem to mind at all. One evening, Albert mentioned that cows and goats digested their food by constantly swallowing it, spitting it back up after acids in one of several stomachs had broken it down, chewing it, and then swallowing again. As his brothers and sisters groaned, Albert noticed his parents squeeze hands affectionately. They were proud of their son, glad that he had found a way to join in evening conversations.

It is a fact of human nature that if you practice something long enough, you get better at it. By the time Albert was nine, he could think of fifteen ways to turn any topic into a discussion of something gross. Mind you, he only had this talent if there was a fork or spoon in his hand and he was sitting at a table with a plate and a glass within easy reach.

By the time Albert was eleven, his twin sisters were living in a dorm at university and the two oldest brothers had taken an apartment together in Toronto and were trying to start their own software company. They wanted to specialize in computer programs which could respond to human voice commands. They wanted computers that could listen.

Even though there were fewer people around the table and Albert didn't need to say something gross to get attention, he couldn't stop himself. By the time he was fifteen years old and starting to date, Albert automatically thought of at least thirty ways to turn any topic into something gross and could not stop himself from saying the top three.

Most people never noticed. Most people never sat down and ate a meal with Albert. At school, he tended to eat his lunch walking around the grounds with friends, or maybe standing and chomping on a slice of pizza. He never sat down.

Norma was the name of Albert's first girlfriend. Dates weren't a particular problem, so long as Albert stuck to movies. Popcorn and a coke didn't count as dinnertime, even though he was sitting and eating food, because watching or listening to something while you ate was never allowed at home.

One day, though, Norma prepared a surprise picnic and the surprise was all hers when Albert spent three hours reciting what ants could and had done to people in South America and Africa.

Irene, his second girlfriend, left him after inviting him to dinner with her family. Irene's father collected spoons inscribed with the names of famous cities of the world. Irene's father showed Albert his collection, and Albert, in return, told him about gruesome crimes and disasters which happened in each one of those cities.

Albert didn't have too many girlfriends after Norma and Irene. People talk.

In his junior year, Alicia Assinder invited Albert out to a movie. He was surprised but happy. Albert had always thought Alicia Assinder was wonderful.

They had a terrific time and, during their first month together, went to three movies, two plays, an amusement park, and four dances before Alicia insisted they have dinner, just the two of them, in a simple little Italian restaurant she knew. Albert winced. Italians used long noodles and red sauces which, to a mind trained to spout gross comments, looked far too much like intestines and gore.

He sighed as he dressed that night. A tear formed in one corner of his left eye. He liked Alicia and was sorry to be losing her.

They sat down, across from each other, glanced at the menu, and ordered.

"I like the spaghetti here," Alicia said.

"If you scrunch wet spaghetti up, into a tight ball, it looks like a brain," said Albert, immediately breaking his vow that he wouldn't say one word during the entire meal, just nod on occasion.

"That's true," said Alicia, "but it's a little too tan. Brains are supposed to be gray. But if you dab on a little tomato sauce, who can tell?"

"If you hold spaghetti up and wiggle it," said Albert, "it can look like one of those tape worms that can get into your body in the tropics. Don't walk around barefooted in the tropics, not with a cut on your foot."

"Tapeworms!" shouted Alicia, causing people at other tables to look and Albert to cringe. He knew he'd gone too far. "You're worried about tapeworms in the tropics? Have you ever heard how you're supposed to escape from an anaconda, one of those big snakes?"

"No," said Albert, surprised.

"They squeeze you first, right? And then they eat you whole and digest you inside their stomachs for about a week or something. Anyway, if an anaconda is coming after you, you're supposed to lie down and pretend you're already dead so the snake won't squeeze you. Then, you dangle a leg in the air so the snake starts swallowing your leg instead of your head. When the snake is half way up your leg and can't move, you spin around and kill it with your knife."

"What if you don't have a knife?" Albert asked, stunned.

"Too bad," said Alicia with a shrug, sipping her drink.

Albert sat in silence for a moment and then slowly said, "Did you know that crocodiles can outrun a person over a short distance? If you're being chased by a crocodile you should run zigzag patterns because crocodiles can't run very well side to side. They're too low to the ground."

"Actually," said Alicia, "I knew that."

"Alicia?"

"Yes?"

"Do you have any brothers and sisters?"

"Four brothers and three sisters," said Alicia with a smile.

"Are you the . . . the youngest?"

"Yes."

"Me too."

"I know," said Alicia. "I know."

Albert smiled, sat back, and waited for his dinner.

Trivial Pursuit

(Being an Investigation into the
Origin of the Word "Trivia")

CLAIRE MACKAY

Oh, the Romans were slick with marble and brick,
With granite, with all things lapideous;
They built bulwarks and bridges with curlicued
    ridges,
And bathtubs quite frequently hideous.

They built villas in valleys and pillars in alleys
And utterly splendid abodes,
And great promenades with grand colonnades –
But mostly they kept building roads.

They built tunnels through mountains and funnels
    for fountains,
And cages for Christians God-fearing;

For Emperor Otto they built a blue grotto
And a *circus* for charioteering.

Then they went slumming and built all the plumbing
In countries that still worshipped toads,
But being the kind with a one-track mind
They never stopped building those roads.

As Rome's flag unfurled over more of the world,
More worried the government grew:
Would people stay loyal, on near and far soil?
Even those with their skin painted blue?

To keep folks connected, not to mention subjected,
And to make sure they all paid their taxes,
The Imperial word must be quickly transferred –
And there weren't any cell phones or faxes.

Then a clever young chap took a look at the map
With its highways fine-patterned as lace,
And he pointed with glee to each junction where
      three
Major roads made a gathering-place.

And he shouted, "Hey guys! It's in front of our eyes!
It's a super idea! It's a winner!

It's a wow! It's a beaut! It's a trivial pursuit,
And we'll get it all done before dinner!

"We can nail up the news and the Emperor's views
On the signposts where three roads converge,
Then let the folks know there's a place they can go
To meet and to mingle and merge.

"We'll write up each rumor, the best bits of humor,
What's hot and what's not and what's arty,
The prices of sandals, the vices of Vandals,
And the annual Ides of March party."

The die was thus cast and picked up pretty fast
By each Julius and every Olivia:
For a late-breaking scoop, or to stay in the loop,
They'd go truckin' on down to the *trivia*.

Have you now figured out how the word came about
From that clever young fellow's idea?
In Latin, you see, three's *tri* (pronounced "tree")
And a road is – you guessed it! – a *via*.

A Second Language

ALICE KANE

A mother Mouse was walking down the road with her little ones around her, and suddenly an enormous Cat appeared. The little mice screamed and tried to hide behind their mother. But the mother turned around bravely, and she faced that Cat, and she said to it, "BOW WOW!" And, as the Cat ran away, she looked at her children and she told them, "Let that be a lesson to you. Never underestimate the value of a second language."

Diana Is Invited to Tea with Tragic Results

L.M. MONTGOMERY

October was a beautiful month at Green Gables, when the birches in the hollow turned as golden as sunshine and the maples behind the orchard were royal crimson and the wild cherry-trees along the lane put on the loveliest shades of dark red and bronzy green, while the fields sunned themselves in aftermaths.

Anne reveled in the world of color about her.

"Oh, Marilla," she exclaimed one Saturday morning, coming dancing in with her arms full of gorgeous boughs, "I'm so glad I live in a world where there are Octobers. It would be terrible if we just skipped from September to November, wouldn't it? Look at these maple branches. Don't they give you a thrill – several thrills? I'm going to decorate my room with them."

"Messy things," said Marilla, whose aesthetic sense was not noticeably developed. "You clutter up your room entirely too much with out-of-doors stuff, Anne. Bedrooms were made to sleep in."

"Oh, and dream in too, Marilla. And you know one can dream so much better in a room where there are pretty things. I'm going to put these boughs in the old blue jug and set them on my table."

"Mind you don't drop leaves all over the stairs then. I'm going to a meeting of the Aid Society at Carmody this afternoon, Anne, and I won't likely be home before dark. You'll have to get Matthew and Jerry their supper, so mind you don't forget to put the tea to draw until you sit down at the table as you did last time."

"It was dreadful of me to forget," said Anne apologetically, "but that was the afternoon I was trying to think of a name for Violet Vale and it crowded other things out. Matthew was so good. He never scolded a bit. He put the tea down himself and said we could wait awhile as well as not. And I told him a lovely fairy story while we were waiting, so he didn't find the time long at all. It was a beautiful fairy story, Marilla. I forgot the end of it, so I made up an end for it myself and Matthew said he couldn't tell where the join came in."

"Matthew would think it all right, Anne, if you took a notion to get up and have dinner in the middle of the night. But you keep your wits about you this time. And – I don't really know if I'm doing right – it may make you more addle-pated than ever – but you can ask Diana to come over and spend the afternoon with you and have tea here."

"Oh, Marilla!" Anne clasped her hands. "How perfectly lovely! You *are* able to imagine things after all or else you'd never have understood how I've longed for that very thing. It will seem so nice and grown-uppish. No fear of my forgetting to put the tea to draw when I have company. Oh, Marilla, can I use the rosebud spray tea-set?"

"No, indeed! The rosebud tea-set! Well, what next? You know I never use that except for the minister or the Aids. You'll put down the old brown tea-set. But you can open the little yellow crock of cherry preserves. It's time it was being used anyhow – I believe it's beginning to work. And you can cut some fruit-cake and have some of the cookies and snaps."

"I can just imagine myself sitting down at the head of the table and pouring out the tea," said Anne, shutting her eyes ecstatically. "And asking Diana if she takes sugar! I know she doesn't but of course I'll ask her just as if I didn't know. And then pressing her to take another piece of fruit-cake and another helping of preserves. Oh, Marilla, it's a wonderful sensation just to think of it. Can I take her into the spare room to lay off her hat when she comes? And then into the parlor to sit?"

"No. The sitting-room will do for you and your company. But there's a bottle half full of raspberry cordial that was left over from the church social the other night. It's on the second shelf of the sitting-room closet and you and Diana can have it if you like, and a cooky to eat with it along in the afternoon, for I daresay Matthew'll be late coming in to tea since he's hauling potatoes to the vessel."

Anne flew down to the hollow, past the Dryad's Bubble and up the spruce path to Orchard Slope, to ask Diana to tea. As a result, just after Marilla had driven off to Carmody, Diana came over, dressed in her second best dress and looking exactly as it is proper to look when asked out to tea. At other times she was wont to run into the kitchen without knocking; but now she knocked primly at the front door. And when Anne, dressed in *her* second best, as primly opened it, both little girls shook hands as gravely as if they had never met before. This unnatural solemnity lasted until after Diana had been taken to the east gable to lay off her hat and then had sat for ten minutes in the sitting-room, toes in position.

"How is your mother?" inquired Anne politely, just as if she had not seen Mrs. Barry picking apples that morning in excellent health and spirits.

"She is very well, thank you. I suppose Mr. Cuthbert is hauling potatoes to the *Lily Sands* this afternoon, is he?" said Diana, who had ridden down to Mr. Harmon Andrews' that morning in Matthew's cart.

"Yes. Our potato crop is very good this year. I hope your father's potato crop is good, too."

"It is fairly good, thank you. Have you picked many of your apples yet?"

"Oh, ever so many," said Anne, forgetting to be dignified and jumping up quickly. "Let's go out to the orchard and get some of the Red Sweetings, Diana. Marilla says we can have all that are left on the tree. Marilla is a very generous woman. She said we could have fruit-cake and cherry preserves for tea. But it isn't good manners to tell your company what you are going to give them to eat, so I won't tell you what she said we could have to drink. Only it begins with an *r* and a *c* and it's a bright red color. I love bright red drinks, don't you? They taste twice as good as any other color."

The orchard, with its great sweeping boughs that bent to the ground with fruit, proved so delightful that the little girls spent most of the afternoon in it, sitting in a grassy corner where the frost had spared the green and the mellow autumn sunshine lingered warmly, eating apples and talking as hard as they could. Diana had much to tell Anne of what went on in school. She had to sit with Gertie Pye and she hated it; Gertie squeaked her pencil all the time and it just made her – Diana's – blood run cold; Ruby Gillis had charmed all her warts away, true's you live, with a magic pebble that old Mary Joe from the Creek gave her. You had to rub the warts with the pebble and then throw it away over your left shoulder at the time of the new moon and the warts would all go. Charlie Sloane's name was written up with Em White's on the porch wall and Em White was *awful mad* about it; Sam Boulter had "sassed" Mr. Phillips in class and Mr. Phillips whipped him and Sam's father came down to the school and dared Mr. Phillips to lay a hand on one of his children again; and Mattie Andrews had a new red hood and a blue crossover with tassels on it and the airs she put on about it were perfectly sickening; and Lizzie Wright didn't speak to Mamie Wilson because Mamie Wilson's grown-up sister had cut out Lizzie Wright's grown-up sister with her beau; and everybody missed Anne so and wished she'd come to school again; and Gilbert Blythe –

But Anne didn't want to hear about Gilbert Blythe. She jumped up hurriedly and said suppose they go in and have some raspberry cordial.

Anne looked on the second shelf of the sitting-room pantry but there was no bottle of raspberry cordial there. Search revealed it away back on the top shelf. Anne put it on a tray and set it on the table with a tumbler.

"Now, please help yourself, Diana," she said politely. "I don't believe I'll have any just now. I don't feel as if I wanted any after all those apples."

Diana poured herself out a tumblerful, looked at its bright red hue admiringly, and then sipped it daintily.

"That's awfully nice raspberry cordial, Anne," she said. "I didn't know raspberry cordial was so nice."

"I'm real glad you like it. Take as much as you want. I'm going to run out and stir the fire up. There are so many responsibilities on a person's mind when they're keeping house, isn't there?"

When Anne came back from the kitchen Diana was drinking her second glassful of cordial; and, being entreated thereto by Anne, she offered no particular objection to the drinking of a third. The tumblerfuls were generous ones and the raspberry cordial was certainly very nice.

"The nicest I ever drank," said Diana. "It's ever so much nicer than Mrs. Lynde's although she brags of hers so much. It doesn't taste a bit like hers."

"I should think Marilla's raspberry cordial would prob'ly be much nicer than Mrs. Lynde's," said Anne loyally. "Marilla is a famous cook. She is trying to teach me to cook but I assure you, Diana, it is uphill work. There's so little scope for imagination in cookery. You just have to go by rules. The last time I made a cake I forgot to put the flour in. I was thinking the loveliest story about you and me, Diana. I thought you were desperately ill with smallpox and everybody deserted you, but I went boldly to your bedside and nursed you back to life; and then I took the smallpox and died and I was buried under those poplar trees in the graveyard and you planted a rose-bush by my grave and watered it with your tears; and you never, never forgot the friend of your youth who sacrificed her life for you. Oh, it was such a pathetic tale, Diana. The tears just rained down over my cheeks while I mixed the cake. But I forgot the flour and the cake was a dismal failure. Flour is so essential to cakes, you know. Marilla was very cross and I don't wonder. I'm a great trial to her. She was terribly mortified about the pudding sauce last week. We had a plum pudding for dinner on Tuesday and there was half the pudding and a pitcherful of sauce left over. Marilla said there was enough for another dinner and told me to set it on the pantry shelf and cover it. I meant to cover it just as much as could be, Diana, but when I carried it in I was imagining I was a nun – of course I'm a Protestant but I imagined I was a Catholic – taking the veil to bury a broken heart in cloistered seclusion; and I forgot all about covering the pudding sauce. I thought of it next morning and ran to the pantry. Diana, fancy if you can my extreme horror at finding a mouse drowned in that pudding sauce! I lifted the mouse out with a spoon and threw it out in the yard and then I washed the spoon in three waters. Marilla was out milking and I fully intended to ask her when she came in if I'd give the sauce to the pigs; but when she did come in I was imagining that I was a frost fairy going through the woods turning the trees red and yellow, whichever they wanted to be, so I never thought about the pudding sauce again and Marilla sent me out to pick apples. Well, Mr. and Mrs. Chester Ross from Spencervale came here that morning. You know they are very stylish people, especially Mrs. Chester Ross. When Marilla called me in, dinner was all ready and everybody was at the table. I tried to be as polite and dignified as I could be, for I wanted Mrs. Chester Ross to think I was a ladylike little girl even if I wasn't pretty. Everything went right until I saw Marilla coming with the plum pudding in one hand and the pitcher of pudding sauce, *warmed up*, in the other. Diana, that was a terrible moment. I remembered everything and I just stood up in my place and shrieked out, 'Marilla, you mustn't use that pudding sauce. There was a mouse drowned in it. I forgot to tell you before.' Oh, Diana, I shall never forget that awful moment if I live to be a hundred. Mrs. Chester

Ross just *looked* at me and I thought I would sink through the floor with mortification. She is such a perfect housekeeper and fancy what she must have thought of us. Marilla turned red as fire but she never said a word – then. She just carried that sauce and pudding out and brought in some strawberry preserves. She even offered me some, but I couldn't swallow a mouthful. It was like heaping coals of fire on my head. After Mrs. Chester Ross went away Marilla gave me a dreadful scolding. Why, Diana, what is the matter?"

Diana had stood up very unsteadily; then she sat down again, putting her hands to her head.

"I'm – I'm awful sick," she said, a little thickly. "I – I – must go right home."

"Oh, you mustn't dream of going home without your tea," cried Anne in distress. "I'll get it right off – I'll go and put the tea down this very minute."

"I must go home," repeated Diana, stupidly but determinedly.

"Let me get you a lunch anyhow," implored Anne. "Let me give you a bit of fruit-cake and some of the cherry preserves. Lie down on the sofa for a little while and you'll be better. Where do you feel bad?"

"I must go home," said Diana, and that was all she would say. In vain Anne pleaded.

"I never heard of company going home without

tea," she mourned. "Oh, Diana, do you suppose that it's possible you're really taking the smallpox? If you are I'll go and nurse you, you can depend on that. I'll never forsake you. But I do wish you'd stay till after tea. Where do you feel bad?"

"I'm awful dizzy," said Diana.

And indeed, she walked very dizzily. Anne, with tears of disappointment in her eyes, got Diana's hat and went with her as far as the Barry yard fence. Then she wept all the way back to Green Gables, where she sorrowfully put the remainder of the raspberry cordial back into the pantry and got tea ready for Matthew and Jerry, with all the zest gone out of the performance.

The next day was Sunday and as the rain poured down in torrents from dawn till dusk Anne did not stir abroad from Green Gables. Monday afternoon Marilla sent her down to Mrs. Lynde's on an errand. In a very short space of time Anne came flying back up the lane, with tears rolling down her cheeks. Into the kitchen she dashed and flung herself face downward on the sofa in an agony.

"Whatever has gone wrong now, Anne?" queried Marilla in doubt and dismay. "I do hope you haven't gone and been saucy to Mrs. Lynde again."

No answer from Anne save more tears and stormier sobs!

"Anne Shirley, when I ask you a question I want to be answered. Sit right up this very minute and tell me what you are crying about."

Anne sat up, tragedy personified.

"Mrs. Lynde was up to see Mrs. Barry to-day and Mrs. Barry was in an awful state," she wailed. "She says that I set Diana *drunk* Saturday and sent her home in a disgraceful condition. And she says I must be a thoroughly bad, wicked little girl and she's never, never going to let Diana play with me again. Oh, Marilla, I'm just overcome with woe."

Marilla stared in blank amazement.

"Set Diana drunk!" she said when she found her voice. "Anne, are you or Mrs. Barry crazy? What on earth did you give her?"

"Not a thing but raspberry cordial," sobbed Anne. "I never thought raspberry cordial would set people drunk, Marilla – not even if they drank three big tumblerfuls as Diana did. Oh, it sounds so – so – like Mrs. Thomas' husband! But I didn't mean to set her drunk."

"Drunk fiddlesticks!" said Marilla, marching to the sitting-room pantry. There on the shelf was a bottle she at once recognized as one containing some of her three year old homemade currant wine for which she was celebrated in Avonlea, although certain of the stricter sort, Mrs. Barry among them, disapproved strongly of it. And at the same time Marilla recollected that she had put the bottle of raspberry cordial down in the cellar instead of in the pantry as she told Anne.

She went back to the kitchen with the wine bottle in hand. Her face was twitching in spite of herself.

"Anne, you certainly have a genius for getting into trouble. You went and gave Diana currant wine instead of raspberry cordial. Didn't you know the difference yourself?"

"I never tasted it," said Anne. "I thought it was the cordial. I meant to be so – so – hospitable. Diana got awfully sick and had to go home. Mrs. Barry told Mrs. Lynde she was simply dead drunk. She just laughed silly like when her mother asked her what was the matter and went to sleep and slept for hours. Her mother smelled her breath and knew she was drunk! She had a fearful headache all day yesterday. Mrs. Barry is so indignant. She will never believe but what I did it on purpose."

"I should think she would better punish Diana for being so greedy as to drink three glassfuls of anything," said Marilla shortly. "Why, three of those big glasses would have made her sick even if it had only been cordial. Well, this story will be a nice handle for those folks who are so down on me for making currant wine, although I haven't made any for three years ever since I found out that the minister didn't approve. I just kept that bottle for sickness. There, there, child, don't cry. I can't see as you were to blame although I'm sorry it happened so."

"I must cry," said Anne. "My heart is broken. The stars in their courses fight against me, Marilla. Diana and I are parted forever. Oh, Marilla, I little dreamed of this when first we swore our vows of friendship."

"Don't be foolish, Anne. Mrs. Barry will think better of it when she finds you're not really to blame. I suppose she thinks you've done it for a silly joke or something of that sort. You'd best go up this evening and tell her how it was."

"My courage fails me at the thought of facing Diana's injured mother," sighed Anne. "I wish you'd go, Marilla. You're so much more dignified than I am. Likely she'd listen to you quicker than to me."

"Well, I will," said Marilla, reflecting that it would probably be the wiser course. "Don't cry any more, Anne. It will be all right."

Marilla had changed her mind about its being all right by the time she got back from Orchard Slope. Anne was watching for her coming and flew to the porch door to meet her.

"Oh, Marilla, I know by your face that it's been no use," she said sorrowfully. "Mrs. Barry won't forgive me?"

"Mrs. Barry, indeed!" snapped Marilla. "Of all the unreasonable women I ever saw she's the worst. I told her it was all a mistake and you weren't to blame, but she just simply didn't believe me. And she rubbed it well in about my currant wine and how I'd always said it couldn't have the least effect on anybody. I just told her plainly that currant wine wasn't meant to be drunk three tumblerfuls at a time and that if a child I had to do with was so greedy I'd sober her up with a right good spanking."

Marilla whisked into the kitchen, grievously disturbed, leaving a very much distracted little soul in the porch behind her. Presently Anne stepped out bare-headed into the chill autumn dusk; very determinedly and steadily she took her way down through the sere clover field over the log bridge and up through the spruce grove, lighted by a pale little moon hanging low over the western woods. Mrs. Barry, coming to the door in answer to a timid knock, found a white-lipped, eager-eyed suppliant on the doorstep.

Her face hardened. Mrs. Barry was a woman of strong prejudices and dislikes, and her anger was of the cold, sullen sort which is always hardest to overcome. To do her justice, she really believed Anne had made Diana drunk out of sheer malice prepense, and she was honestly anxious to preserve her little daughter from the contamination of further intimacy with such a child.

"What do you want?" she said stiffly.

Anne clasped her hands.

"Oh, Mrs. Barry, please forgive me. I did not mean to – to – intoxicate Diana. How could I? Just imagine if you were a poor little orphan girl that kind people had adopted and you had just one bosom friend in all the world. Do you think you would intoxicate her on purpose? I thought it was only raspberry cordial. I was firmly convinced it was raspberry cordial. Oh, please don't say that you won't let Diana play with me any more. If you do you will cover my life with a dark cloud of woe."

This speech, which would have softened good Mrs. Lynde's heart in a twinkling, had no effect on Mrs. Barry except to irritate her still more. She was suspicious of Anne's big words and dramatic gestures and imagined that the child was making fun of her. So she said, coldly and cruelly:

"I don't think you are a fit little girl for Diana to associate with. You'd better go home and behave yourself."

Anne's lip quivered.

"Won't you let me see Diana just once to say farewell?" she implored.

"Diana has gone over to Carmody with her father," said Mrs. Barry, going in and shutting the door.

Anne went back to Green Gables calm with despair.

"My last hope is gone," she told Marilla. "I went up and saw Mrs. Barry myself and she treated me very insultingly. Marilla, I do *not* think she is a well-bred woman. There is nothing more to do except to pray and I haven't much hope that that'll do much good because, Marilla, I do not believe that God Himself can do very much with such an obstinate person as Mrs. Barry."

"Anne, you shouldn't say such things," rebuked Marilla, striving to overcome that unholy tendency to laughter which she was dismayed to find growing upon her. And indeed, when she told the whole story to Matthew that night, she did laugh heartily over Anne's tribulations.

But when she slipped into the east gable before going to bed and found that Anne had cried herself to sleep, an unaccustomed softness crept into her face.

"Poor little soul," she murmured, lifting a loose curl of hair from the child's tear-stained face. Then she bent down and kissed the flushed cheek on the pillow.

A Palace for Aberbog

SARAH ELLIS

The seaside town of Aberbog was not an important place. It had never been the site for an Expo. It had never hosted a winter fair or a summer festival. It didn't have a wax museum or a mall or a giant water slide, so it didn't attract many visitors. And it had certainly never been visited by royalty.

Everyone was very surprised, therefore, when the rider arrived. He was a young man dressed in blue satin with fine high black boots and he rode into town on a shiny bay horse. Shopkeepers stood outside their doors staring and people's heads popped out of windows all along the main road, but the rider looked neither left nor right. He cantered to the town square, pulled a notice out of his saddlebag and nailed it to the large oak tree. Then he rode out the other end of town. But nobody saw him leave because they were too busy reading.

READ YE, READ YE

Notice is hereby given and posted that the esteemed Count Filbert does shortly plan to begin construction of a new summer palace of great elegance and splendor. The site for this edifice will be chosen on the basis of a

CONTEST.

Esteemed Count Filbert will visit each of the coastal towns in turn and the town that can provide the best

ENTERTAINMENT

will be honored as the site for the glorious new palace.

"New palace?" harrumphed Betty Pringle, the town printer. "What does Filbert need a new palace for? He's already got five."

"Oh, he just doesn't like to clean them," said Perkins the fisherman. "As soon as the fireplaces get sooty and the tapestries need a scrub he abandons that palace and builds a new one."

"It's my belief," said Mary the baker, "that his mother is behind it all. That Countess Ornella, she just keeps changing her mind about what style she wants. One year it's all clouds and angels, and then as soon as it's finished she wants the ancient Egyptian look."

"Well, he's got quite a nerve just announcing that he's coming by to be entertained," said Jones the farmer. "Sounds like an excuse for a bunch of free meals to me."

Jones's grumpiness was contagious.

"Yes, who does he think he is, anyway?"

"Not so much as a by-your-leave."

"He's not the boss of us."

As the Count traveled down the coast, news reached Aberbog of the entertainments that the other towns had provided. Betty printed reports in the *Aberbog Sometimes News*: operas, banquets, rodeos, trapeze acts, fireworks. The people of Aberbog made no plans at all.

"Hey, listen to this," said Martin the musician. "In Snikville they served him a dessert that was a watermelon stuffed with a honeydew stuffed with a cantaloupe stuffed with an orange stuffed with a plum stuffed with a gooseberry stuffed with a raisin."

Mary snorted. "I hope he doesn't think he's going to get that sort of treatment here. Good plain food is all we'll be having. He'll have to take us as he finds us."

The Count arrived in Aberbog at noon on a Wednesday. Nobody cared two hoots about him, but they all found a reason to be in the square to watch his arrival nonetheless.

The coach was beautiful, shining gold in the sun and pulled by four midnight-black horses with reins of red velvet. The chief footman, a man with a pinched little mouth and a razor-sharp nose, descended from the carriage and enquired, "Where is the welcoming party? Where are the dignitaries? Where is the band, the red carpet, the small shy child with a bouquet of flowers?"

"We haven't got any of that," said Perkins.

"Oh, thank goodness," said a voice from inside the coach. And out climbed the Count. He was skinny and pale and tall. "Off you go," he said to the coachman and all the retinue. "Go away somewhere and pick me up tonight."

With that the Count gave a little nod to the people, walked over to the town square, sat down with his back against the oak tree, kicked off his shoes, gave a sigh, and closed his eyes. The coach and horses pulled away.

Betty's face softened. "Oh, that poor boy. He looks tuckered out. We should just let him rest."

So the Aberbogians took one good stare at the Count and then went about their business. Nobody approached the royal visitor except Fred the cat, who curled up on the Count's lap and went to sleep as well.

After a couple of hours Mary happened to look out the bakery window and saw that the Count was looking around, rubbing his eyes and stretching.

"I wonder if he's had lunch," she thought. She wandered out into the square and approached the young man. "Excuse me," she said. "Would you like a bun?"

"Is it stuffed with anything?" asked the Count.

"No," said Mary, her heart sinking.

"Does it have a sauce on it?" asked the Count.

"No, it's just plain, I'm afraid," said Mary.

"Can I eat it here, out of my hand?" asked the Count.

"Sure," said Mary.

"Then yes, *please*," said the Count.

As is usually the way in Aberbog one thing led to another and people found excuses to leave their work and wander down to the square. The whole town ended up spending the rest of the afternoon lounging around and chatting. Nancy let the Count play with baby Barnaby. Barnaby grinned and pulled the Count's nose and spit up, but just a little bit and the Count didn't seem to mind.

Jones, who was a champion knitter in his spare time, showed the Count plain knit and purl and the Count made an afghan square. Betty told riddles and knock-knock jokes. The Count hadn't heard any of them. Everyone made daisy chains. Martin taught the Count three chords on the banjo and the royal visitor joined in on a rousing chorus of "Skunk in the Teakettle."

Skunk in the teakettle, twelve by twelve,
If you want more verses, sing 'em yerself.

"Yee-hah," yelled the Count and then turned bright red.

When the day got cooler the people divided into two teams for baseball. The Count was the first chosen and he turned bright red again.

Running backwards for a fly ball in the seventh inning he tripped over a molehill and landed flat on his back. The ball fell into his glove. "Way to go, Stretch," yelled a voice from the sidelines. And so the Count got a nickname.

For dinner there was a pot-luck and then Stretch helped wash the dishes. He got the giggles and broke a few glasses but nobody minded. Then everyone sat around with cups of tea and told ghost stories. Stretch told a real goose-bumper about a chain-clanging headless phantom who was his own great-great-uncle.

When his carriage arrived Stretch didn't want to leave. But there were hugs all around and promises to write. Jones gave Stretch a knitted tea cozy and off he went, wearing the wilted daisy chain around his neck, and waving until the carriage pulled out of sight.

The townspeople all agreed that they had been wrong about the Count, that he was a good sort, fitted right in, and that there should be more like him. Then they more or less forgot about him and about the new palace.

They were flabbergasted, therefore, when a notice arrived, all printed on parchment, with ribbons and seals, informing the town that Aberbog had won the contest. The new palace was to be built on Windy Hill, just to the north of town.

"Oh no," said Nancy. "Windy Hill is our best skateboarding place. What can we do? This is an emergency."

Everyone agreed.

"This is a catastrophe."

"This is a disaster!"

"Keep calm," said Martin. "I've got an idea. I think Mary is right, that Countess Ornella is behind all this. And I've got a pretty good notion how we can stop it." He described his plan to the others and together they composed a letter to the Countess, the letter that could save Windy Hill.

Countess Ornella was delighted to get an invitation to visit Aberbog. "How quaint," she said to the Count. "I'll wear my country clothes so that I fit right in, and I'll be charming to all those dear simple people. What a thrill it will be for them to meet me." The Count did not reply.

For the next few weeks the people of the town of Aberbog worked tirelessly to prepare for the forth-coming visit. They had work parties, meetings, committees, and rehearsals. They organized, delegated, assigned, and cooperated.

The day finally dawned. Countess Ornella arrived, dressed as a shepherdess with a pink flouncy dress with lace overskirt, white stockings and shoes, ringlets, and a crook. She was escorted immediately to the town hall where the entertainment was planned.

Betty sat her in the seat of honor and Jones gave a long speech of welcome. He used a lot of words like "notwithstanding" and "for the nonce." His voice came out as even as toothpaste but the Countess was used to this kind of talk and she just smiled and thought about whether her bedroom in the new palace should be painted icicle green with écru trim or that divine new double café-latte shade.

She began to notice, however, that the seat of honor was very high. Her feet were starting to get pins and needles from not touching the floor. And she also thought that the town hall was rather hot and stuffy. She didn't know, of course, that fires had been burning in the fireplaces all morning to create just that effect.

At long last Jones finished and he introduced Perkins who introduced Mary who introduced Martin who introduced little Peggy Ramsay.

"And now the moment we've all been waiting for, Peggy Ramsay and her presentation on the life cycle of the newt! Can somebody close those drapes, please? Thank you. Take it away, Peggy!"

Little Peggy Ramsay knew everything about the newt and she had slides. Hundreds of slides. The dim room was hot and airless. Some of the slides were upside down.

After the newts, Jones announced a comedy act. "Thank heavens," thought the Countess, who was beginning to twitch.

Peter the potter came on stage and sat on a high stool. "I have a joke," he announced. He spoke very slowly, spacing his words carefully. "Once there was this rowboat with three men in it. One was a shoe-maker, one was a carpenter and one was . . . Oh, I've just forgotten what the third one was. Okay. I'll start again. Once there was a rowboat with two men in it. One was a shoemaker. One was a . . . No, hold it. I made a small mistake. It wasn't a rowboat. It was a sailboat. I'll start again. Once there was a sailboat with three men in it . . ."

Countess Ornella's eyes glazed over and her neck started to hurt. Just when she felt her head flopping forward a round of applause woke her up. Peter was bowing.

Jones returned to the stage. "Now, back by popular acclaim, put your hands together please for – The Aberbog Children's Chorus!"

The Countess felt slightly better. "Children," she thought. "That gives me a chance to smile and look sweet, as though I love children." But her heart sank when the first lines of the song reached her:

Ninety-nine bottles of beer on the wall,
Ninety-nine bottles of beer . . .

Ninety-nine bottles of beer later Countess Ornella felt as though she had lived her whole life in Aberbog Town Hall. And it wasn't over. Jones thanked the Countess so much for coming and said how much they were looking forward to her attending many such events when she lived in their neighborhood.

"Our next offering is going to be a pageant of the history of Aberbog, from prehistoric times to the present."

The Countess reached a decision. She hopped down from the seat of honor onto her prickly feet and announced, "Oh, you dear sweet people. We have enjoyed ourselves greatly but the heavy duties of our noble position force us to leave you now. A fond farewell." Then she retrieved her shepherdess crook, gathered up her lacy skirts, and fled.

The people of Aberbog were quiet until they heard the sound of Countess Ornella's horses clip-clopping out of town. Then they burst out of the hall, leapt and laughed and whooped their way to the beach. They took off their shoes and ran into the sea with their clothes on. They played water tag and did bellyflops off each other's shoulders. They launched a submarine sea monster attack on Jones and dunked him. They constructed new hairstyles out of seaweed. Then they shouted three cheers for Martin, and all went home for dinner.

Aberbog never did hear any further plans for a palace on Windy Hill. A little while after the contest deadline they heard a rumor that something grand was being constructed in Snikville. Countess Ornella never found another occasion to visit. But Stretch dropped by from time to time, on his motorcycle. Everyone was always glad to see him. He never got very good at knitting or the banjo or washing dishes. But he sure could pick those fly balls out of the air.

Soothing the Savage Beast

BILL RICHARDSON

Curtis headed home from school and dawdled on
   his way,
His face was frozen in a kind of glower.
When all his friends were finally freed to run and
   shout and play,
He wrestled the piano for an hour.

Each day he had to sit astride the hard revolving stool,
Each day he had to practice without fail.
Each day it was the same routine when he came in
   from school:
First the major, then the minor scales.

Each day he had to memorize a little piece by Bach,
Or Mozart, or another of that crowd.

His grandma watched his progress with the keenness
   of a hawk;
She told him that one day he'd make her proud.

"When you grow up, you'll thank me," she would
   tell him when he whined,
"To have a skill you ought not be without!
Music is the food of love, and love can be sublime!"
"I think love sucks!" said Curtis, with a pout.

Now on the day of which I speak, as Curtis
   scuffed along –
Not eager in the slightest to begin –
He paused beside a manhole and, as he was
   feeling strong,
He pried the cover off and bellowed in:

"Is anybody home?" he called. His question
   echoed deep.
"Is anybody home?" came back again.
He bellowed in the sewer, "Go and take a flying leap!"
A hand reached up and pulled him down the drain.

He had no time to call for help or raise a loud alarm,
He passed from light to darkness in a trice.
He found himself encircled by a slimy, scaly arm:
Strong as a gorilla, cold as ice.

All was gloom and smelliness. They made a fast
    descent,
The atmosphere was dangerous and rank.
They veered along canals that seemed, no matter
    where they went,
Cold and clammy, dismal, dark, and dank.

Now, you might well suspect that Curtis felt a
    tad distressed,
He didn't know by what he'd just been snatched:
He only knew he didn't feel particularly blessed
At having been abducted down the hatch.

What sewer demon held him in this chill and
    steely grasp?
Was this some evil creature of the night?
When at last they stopped the boy released a
    startled gasp:
They'd come upon a chamber filled with light.

Chandeliers hung everywhere. A thousand candles
    burned,
The room they lit had never seen the sun.
It held a lavish table. Curtis very quickly learned
The reason it was only set for one.

"Of course, you'll stay for dinner," were the words his
  captor said,
And all about the room that sentence rang.
Curtis turned and took him in. His eyes were
  brilliant red:
Red as well, the stains upon his fangs.

Eyes and fangs and scales and tail and breath to
  make you swoon,
And hair that hung about in twisted coils:
The creature said, "Sit down. Relax. I'm having
  dinner soon.
You're small and shouldn't take too long to boil.

"My microwave is broken, but the kettle's
  working well.
There'll only be the shortest of delays.
In the meantime, have a seat and visit for a spell –
Unless, of course, you think you'd like to play?"

He gestured to the corner where a grand piano stood.
Curtis felt a sudden sense of calm.
He said, "Why, yes, I'll play a while. My granny says
  I'm good.
Perhaps you'd like to hear a bit of Brahms?"

The demon clapped his filthy paws, with loud
    delight he trilled,
"Brahms! My favorite! What a clever guy!"
Curtis sat and summoned up his every ounce of will:
He played the very famous lullaby.

"Charming!" said the demon. Curtis played it one
    time through,
He played it twice, then version three and four.
He played it several dozen times, for in his heart
    he knew
Eventually he'd hear the demon snore.

"How lovely!" said his captor, as his lids began to sag.
"Divine!" he said while covering a yawn.
"Oh dear," he said, "I must confess, I feel a trifle
    bagged!
"I'll rest my eyes . . ." In seconds, he was gone.

Enterprising Curtis rose, then quickly as he dared
He fled the room and plunged into the black,
He only thought to gain sufficient distance from
    the lair:
He never once considered looking back.

He followed awful corridors, he twisted left and right,
He prayed a prayer and never words were truer,

Asking for deliverance from the creature of
　　the night,
Rescue from the Phantom of the Sewer.

To make a long, long story short – he found that
　　selfsame hole.
He scuttled up, and hurried down the street,
Squinting in the sunlight like a subterranean mole,
And smelling far from what you might call sweet.

And from that day to this one he has practiced
　　without fail.
When next he meets a beast whose feet are cloven,
He'll know a dozen lullabies to charm him and
　　regale:
Schumann, Schubert, Mozart and Beethoven.

The Hockey Sweater

ROCH CARRIER

The winters of my childhood were long, long seasons. We lived in three places – the school, the church and the skating-rink – but our real life was on the skating-rink. Real battles were won on the skating-rink. Real strength appeared on the skating-rink. The real leaders showed themselves on the skating-rink.

School was a sort of punishment. Parents always want to punish their children and school is their most natural way of punishing us. However, school was also a quiet place where we could prepare for the next hockey game, lay out our next strategies.

As for church, we found there the tranquillity of God: there we forgot school and dreamed about the next hockey game. Through our daydreams it might happen that we would recite a prayer: we would ask God to help us play as well as Maurice Richard.

I remember very well the winter of 1946. We all wore the same uniform as Maurice Richard, the red, white and blue uniform of the Montreal Canadiens, the best hockey team in the world. We all combed our hair like Maurice Richard, and to keep it in place we used a kind of glue – a great deal of glue. We laced our skates like Maurice Richard, we taped our sticks like Maurice Richard. We cut his pictures out of all the newspapers. Truly, we knew everything there was to know about him.

On the ice, when the referee blew his whistle the two teams would rush at the puck; we were five Maurice Richards against five other Maurice Richards, throwing themselves on the puck. We were ten players all wearing the uniform of the Montreal Canadiens, all with the same burning enthusiasm. We all wore the famous number 9 on our backs.

How could we forget that!

One day, my Montreal Canadiens sweater was too small for me; and it was ripped in several places. My mother said: "If you wear that old sweater, people are going to think we are poor!"

Then she did what she did whenever we needed new clothes. She started to look through the catalog

ROCH CARRIER

that the Eaton company in Montreal sent us in the mail every year. My mother was proud. She never wanted to buy our clothes at the general store. The only clothes that were good enough for us were the latest styles from Eaton's catalog. My mother did not like the order forms included in the catalog. They were written in English and she did not understand a single word of it. To order my hockey sweater, she did what she always did. She took out her writing pad and wrote in her fine schoolteacher's hand: "Dear Monsieur Eaton, Would you be so kind as to send me a Canadiens' hockey sweater for my son, Roch, who is ten years old and a little bit tall for his age? Docteur Robitaille thinks he is a little too thin. I am sending you three dollars. Please send me the change if there is any. I hope your packing will be better than it was last time."

Monsieur Eaton answered my mother's letter promptly. Two weeks later we received the sweater.

That day I had one of the greatest disappointments of my life! Instead of the red, white and blue Montreal Canadiens sweater, Monsieur Eaton had sent the blue and white sweater of the Toronto Maple Leafs. I had always worn the red, white and blue sweater of the Montreal Canadiens. All my friends wore the red, white and blue sweater. Never had anyone in my village worn the Toronto sweater. Besides, the Toronto team was always being beaten by the Canadiens.

With tears in my eyes, I found the strength to say: "I'll never wear that uniform."

"My boy," said my mother, "first you're going to try it on! If you make up your mind about something before you try it, you won't go very far in this life."

My mother had pulled the blue and white Toronto Maple Leafs sweater over my head and put my arms into the sleeves. She pulled the sweater down and carefully smoothed the maple leaf right in the middle of my chest.

I was crying. "I can't wear that."

"Why not? This sweater is a perfect fit."

"Maurice Richard would never wear it."

"You're not Maurice Richard! Besides, it's not what you put on your back that matters, it's what you put inside your head."

"You'll never make me put in my head to wear a Toronto Maple Leafs sweater."

My mother sighed in despair and explained to me: "If you don't keep this sweater which fits you perfectly I'll have to write to Monsieur Eaton and explain that you don't want to wear the Toronto sweater. Monsieur Eaton understands French perfectly, but he's English and he's going to be insulted because he likes the Maple Leafs. If he's insulted, do you think he'll be in a hurry to answer us? Spring will come before you play a single game, just because you don't want to wear that nice blue sweater."

So, I had to wear the Toronto Maple Leafs sweater.

When I arrived at the skating rink in my blue sweater, all the Maurice Richards in red, white and blue came, one by one, and looked at me. The referee blew his whistle and I went to take my usual position. The coach came over and told me I would be on the second line. A few minutes later the second line was called; I jumped onto the ice. The Maple Leafs sweater weighed on my shoulders like a mountain. The captain came and told me to wait, he'd need me later, on defense.

By the third period I still had not played.

Then one of the defensemen was hit on the nose with a stick and it started to bleed. I jumped onto the ice. My moment had come!

The referee blew his whistle and gave me a penalty. He said there were already five players on the ice. That was too much! It was too unfair! "This is persecution!" I shouted. "It's just because of my blue sweater!"

I crashed my stick against the ice so hard that it broke.

I bent down to pick up the pieces. When I got up, the young curate, on skates, was standing in front of me.

"My child," he said, "just because you're wearing a new Toronto Maple Leafs sweater, it doesn't mean you're going to make the laws around here. A good boy never loses his temper. Take off your skates and go to the church and ask God to forgive you."

Wearing my Maple Leafs sweater I went to the church, where I prayed to God.

I asked God to send me right away, a hundred million moths that would eat up my Toronto Maple Leafs sweater.

The Grade Five Lie

JEAN LITTLE

I was eating my porridge when Hugh, hurrying too fast, fell down the back stairs. Before Mother could get up, he limped in, sniffling slightly, and displayed a bumped elbow for her inspection. Mother examined it gravely.

"A slight hematoma," she said in a serious voice. "And an abrasion almost invisible to the naked eye. You'll live."

Hugh, who always recovered with the speed of light and who won Mother's admiration with his bravery, chuckled at the impressive words.

"What does that mean?" he asked.

"A little bruise and a scrape I can hardly see."

I glowered at my oatmeal. Why did she have to smile at him like that? He was not so special. I searched my mind for something terrible he had done that I could tell her about.

"Jean, hurry up or you'll be late," Grandma said.

I did not want to go to school. We were going to have another mental arithmetic test, and I still did not know my times tables. If only I could fall down and break my leg . . .

Four-year-old Pat grinned at me.

"Huwwy up, Jean," she parroted. "You'll be late."

I wanted to slap the wide smile off her silly little face. Instead I scooped up a few drops of milk on the tip of my spoon and let fly. The tiny bit of milk splashed her on the nose. I laughed. Before anyone could stop her, Pat grabbed up her mug filled to the brim with milk and sent its entire contents sloshing over me, soaking me to the skin.

The next thing I knew, I was back upstairs changing out of my wet serge dress, cotton petticoat, long brown stockings and underwear into clean dry clothes. Not only was this going to make me really late, but Mother handed me the knitted suit Aunt Gretta had made for my tenth birthday. The ribbed blue skirt was sewn onto a sleeveless cotton vest. Over it went a horizontally striped blue and pink sweater with short sleeves. Nobody else in Miss Marr's class had a homemade knitted suit anything like it.

"I can't wear it," I said in anguished tones.

"It's lovely," my mother said calmly. "Gretta worked hard to make it for you. Don't be ridiculous. Of course you will wear it."

In ten minutes I was gobbling toast and honey, gulping down milk and hating my cheerful little sister who was the cause of all the trouble and who got to stay home and be spoiled by everybody.

When I reached the street, it was ominously quiet. I really was going to be late, and it was all Pat's fault. I ran the first three blocks, but slowed down when I got a stitch in my side. There was still not a single child in sight.

As I passed St. John's School, I could hear the grade four class singing "God Save the King." I sent the small building a look of longing. Mr. Johnston had not had these horrid mental arithmetic tests.

Then I stood stock still. When I got to school, Miss Marr would tell me to put my name on the board to stay after four. I didn't mind staying late – lots of the others got detentions – I wasn't sure what to write, though I had a strong suspicion that you did not write out your whole name. Did you just write your initials? Or one initial and your surname? Or your first name and your last initial?

I had to get it right. The others still called me names when no teacher was near enough to hear. The only game I had ever been invited to play was Crack the

Whip, and they always made me go on the end. Then, when the big girl at the front swung everybody around in a long *Crack!*, I ended up flying through the air and landing with a jarring crash on my hands and knees. As I picked myself up, I'd try to look as though I thought crash-landings were fun. Nobody was fooled.

If I wrote my name up there differently than the others did, they would have a new thing to tease me about. I could hear the jeering voices already.

"You're not just cross-eyed, you're so *dumb* you don't even know how to write your name on the board!"

I stood there, thinking hard. How could I save myself? Once in a while, when a child brought a note from home, he got out of putting his name on the board. Well, my mother would not write me a note.

Perhaps, if your parents were not at home, and some emergency cropped up and you had to deal with it, Miss Marr just might let you sit down without asking for a note. It would have to be a desperate emergency . . .

I began to walk again, taking my time. I had to invent the most convincing lie of my life. Bit by bit, I worked it out. As I imagined how it must have happened, it grew so real that I began to believe it myself. I had every detail ready as I turned the last corner. Then I began to run.

I knew it was essential that I be out of breath when I arrived.

I dashed up the stairs, puffing hard. I opened the door, said a private prayer for help, and entered the grade five classroom. Miss Marr was at her desk. Out of the corner of my eye, I could see monitors collecting the test papers. So far so good.

"Jean," said my teacher, "you're late."

"Yes," I panted, facing her and opening my eyes wide so that I would look innocent and pitiful. "I know. I couldn't help it."

"Why are you late?" she asked.

I took a deep breath.

"Well, I was all ready in plenty of time. But just as I was going out the door, the telephone rang. I knew I should not go back to answer it, but you know my mother and father are both doctors and I was afraid it might be an emergency."

Miss Marr opened her mouth to ask a question, but I rushed on, not giving her time to get a word in edge-wise.

"The trouble was, you see, that nobody was home but me. So I took the receiver off the hook and I said, 'Dr. Littles' residence.'"

Everybody was listening now, even the boys who never paid attention. I kept going.

"MY DAUGHTER IS DYING! MY DAUGHTER IS DYING!"

I saw my teacher jump as I shrieked the words at the top of my lungs. Her eyes were wide with shock. The class gasped. I did not stop for effect. I could not give the teacher time to interrupt.

"It was a man's voice. He sounded frantic with worry. 'I'm sorry,' I told him, 'my parents are out. If you call back, they should be home in one hour.' 'No! Please, don't hang up,' he begged. 'You must come and save her life. If I wait for your parents, she will surely die.' 'Well, I guess if she is dying, I'd better come. Where do you live?' I asked him. '111 King Street,' he told me."

Miss Marr did not even try to ask a question as I paused to catch my breath. The entire class was sitting spellbound. The silence was absolute. Not a desk seat squeaked. Not a giggle broke the hush.

"I hurried in and got the right medicine from the office and then I ran out the door. I didn't go the long way around by the Norwich Street bridge. I was afraid it would take too long. I went down London Road and across some stepping stones down there. When I got to King Street, there was the house. It was a log cabin with wind whistling through the cracks. And as I came up to it, I saw the door was standing open and there were a bunch of people in the doorway and they were all crying. 'What's wrong?' I asked them. 'You are too late,' they sobbed. 'She's dead already.'"

This time, as I snatched a breath, Miss Marr choked back a small sound. She made no attempt to stem the flood of my story. I pressed on.

"'Oh, I am so sorry,' I told them. 'Take me to see her.' So they took me into the cabin and there lay the girl on a trundle bed. Her face was blue and her eyes had rolled up till you could just see white and her teeth were clenched. And her fingers and toes all curled over backwards."

I watched Miss Marr carefully at this point, because I was not absolutely sure what a dead person looked like. The last bit worried me especially. I had heard someone say that when people died, they turned their toes up. That could only mean that their toes curled over backwards, but I was not sure about the fingers.

Miss Marr's face quivered a little and her mouth twitched, but she did not speak. I hurried, eager to finish. It would be a relief to sit down. Even so, in spite of myself, I kept putting in extra bits as they occurred to me.

"'She's not quite dead,' I cried. 'She's just on the point of death. I think I can save her.' I hit her chin and her mouth opened. I poured in the medicine.

She fluttered her lashes and turned a normal color and said weakly, 'Where am I?' I turned and hurried toward the door. But before I could escape, all the weeping people went down on their knees and grabbed hold of my skirt and they said, 'You saved her life! We want to give you a reward. Gold, silver, a bag of emeralds, a horse that will come when you whistle . . . tell us the one thing you want more than anything else in the world and you can have it.'"

I paused for effect this time. I knew no one would break the hush. I wanted my teacher to take in the next bit.

"'The one thing I want more than anything else in the world,' I told them, 'is to be on time for school.' So they let me go and I ran down the hill and across the stepping stones. When I got to the third last stone, though, I slipped and fell in the river and cut my knee. I had to get to shore, go home and bandage my knee and put on dry clothes. Then I hurried here as fast as I could. And that is why I am late."

There was a stunned silence in the classroom. Miss Marr and I stared at each other for a long, long minute. I waited for her to tell me to write my name on the board. Instead she pointed her finger at my desk. Speaking extremely slowly and wearily, she said, "Take . . . your . . . seat. Just . . . take . . . your . . . seat."

I tried to keep a solemn expression on my face. But

it was hard not to grin. I sat down and did not turn my head as a buzz of whispers broke out behind me. I had missed the mental arithmetic test. I had not had to write my name on the board. And I had kept every single person transfixed with my exciting story.

At least three blissful minutes went by before I realized I had no cut on my knee and no bandage, either. Not only that, but I could not remember whether I had told her which knee I was supposed to have cut.

She had believed me. I was sure of that. Yet any second she was going to discover that I had told her a stupendous lie.

I hooked one knee over the other and clasped my hands around the knee on top. I spent the entire morning that way. When I was required to write, I used only one hand. Miss Marr did not ask me a direct question. When recess time came and she said, "Class, stand," I stayed where I was.

"Jean, aren't you going out for recess?" she asked when the others had marched out and there I still sat.

"Oh, Miss Marr," I said in my smallest, most pathetic voice, "I am so tired from saving that girl's life that I have to stay in and have a rest."

Still clutching my knee with both hands, I laid my head down on my desk and shut my eyes.

She did not say a word.

At noon, when she had her back turned, I ran out of the classroom, dashed home, sneaked Band-Aids from my parents' office and plastered them over both knees, to be on the safe side. When I returned to school, Miss Marr smiled and did not ask why both my knees were bandaged.

I sat through the afternoon thinking over what had happened. Did she really guess? The other kids did not seem to have figured out that I had lied. One girl had even smiled at me, as though she might be my friend. Nobody in my class had called me cross-eyed. A boy in grade seven had, though. If only I could shut him up the way I had hushed everybody that morning.

Then I remembered Hugh's knee. That night I asked Mother, "What are the long words for what's wrong with my eyes?"

I was standing beside her chair. She looked up at me.

"Why?" she asked.

"I want to know, that's all. They call me cross-eyed. I want to know the long words, the ones doctors use."

She rhymed off a whole list.

"Say it again. Slowly."

"Strabismus, nystagmus, corneal opacities and eccentric pupils."

I practiced.

The next day I was late coming out of school. The

same grade-seven boy was waiting for me. He had his first snowball ready.

"Cross-eyed, cross-eyed," he chanted and waited for me to start running so that he could chase me, pelting me with hard-packed snowballs.

I turned on him instead.

"I am not cross-eyed," I said in a strong, clear voice. "I have corneal opacities and eccentric pupils."

I glared at him as I spoke, and my eyes were as crossed as ever. But he was so surprised that he stood there, his mouth gaping open like a fish's.

Then I turned my back and walked away. Perhaps his aim was off because he was so used to firing his missiles at a running target. But the first snowball flew past me harmlessly. The second exploded with a smack against a nearby tree.

I kept walking, chin in the air.

In the last two days, I had learned a lot about the power of words. Snowballs would hit me again and I would run away and cry. I would be late and, eventually, I would even have to write my name on the board.

But I had found out what mere words could do. I would not forget.

Jimmy Lorris

LOIS SIMMIE

A quiet little genius,
Whose name was Jimmy Lorris,
Was hooked on reading everything,
But mostly his thesaurus.
He read it through and through and through,
All of his own volition;
Committed it to memory too,
The new enlarged edition.

Now every time he opens up
His mouth he gets in trouble;
Synonyms keep floating out
Like someone blowing bubbles.
At first this really pleased his folks,
Appealing to their vanity;

Then they said if he didn't stop
He'd drive them to insanity.

Father said at dinnertime
He was feeling rather low,
His income down, inflation up,
And business somewhat slow.
"Poor Dad," said Jim, "business is tardy,
Sluggish, humdrum, gradual, slack,
Languid, leaden, passive, backward –"
His mom gave him a smack.

"Jimmy," implored his father,
"Don't *do* that all the time.
Mommy's getting nervous,
She's no longer in her prime."
"Is Mom nervous, timid, irritable,
Hysterical, shaky, aghast,
Apprehensive, restless, shocked,
A nervous wreck at last?"

His mother screamed and tore her hair
And wrung her hands and feet;
"Shut up!" she yelled, "you rotten kid,
You yappy little creep!"
With his hand upon his Roget
A solemn oath Jim swore:

"Not one synonym will cross my lips,
Not one, no, nevermore.

"Are you happy, gratified, satisfied,
Gladdened, delighted, cheered?"
His mom leapt over the table,
And the look in her eyes was weird.
As she led little Jimmy out in the yard
Father heard her say . . .
"Kill. Butcher. Slaughter. Dispatch.
Assassinate. Massacre. Slay."

My Little Brother

My little brother on the bus
Got sat on by a shopper
With lots and lots of parcels,
An umbrella and a hat.

My little brother's real polite,
My little brother's thin and white;
My little brother's quiet,

And my little brother's flat.

Kenny's Canadian History

BRIAN DOYLE

My friend Kenny never seems to wind up in between. In school, anyway. Kenny's either first or last. Me, I'm always in between. So you might say that Kenny and I cover all the spots available. First, last, and in between.

For instance, last week we have two tests in geometry. On the first test I get 75 and Kenny gets *zip*. On the second test I get 75 again and Kenny gets 100.

Our teacher, Shredder, who also teaches us History, can't stand this. It drives him crazy. The Ninja Turtle freaks in the class named him Shredder. To me he's more like Darth Vader. That is, he sounds like Darth Vader. He doesn't look like Darth Vader. He looks more like Daffy Duck.

As I was saying, Shredder can't stand this first or

last business with Kenny. To begin with, Shredder figures that Kenny must have cheated. How can you know absolutely nothing about geometry on Tuesday and absolutely everything about geometry on Wednesday? But he has to give up on the cheating idea because nobody else gets anywhere near 100, so how could Kenny have cheated?

Next, Shredder thinks Kenny's doing it on purpose. Doing it to bug him. This is not true, either. Kenny's not doing this first-last thing to bug Shredder. Kenny doesn't care enough about Shredder to want to bug him. To Kenny, Shredder hardly even exists.

But Shredder can't leave it alone. He gives us one of his "what kind of a person" speeches.

"What kind of a person would deliberately get absolutely nothing, I mean *nothing, diddley squat*, on a geometry test one day and then turn around the next day and score perfect on another geometry test? What kind of a person would you say that was? Mm? Would that be the kind of a person who was perhaps trying to seek attention? To show off perhaps? Is that the kind of a person we are perhaps dealing with here? Does anyone have any opinions on what kind of a person that would be? Get *zilch* on a test one day and 100 the next? Mmm? Any opinions?"

You can tell Shredder is trying to get Kenny back for this. He probably thinks his tests are being made fun of. What kind of a report-card mark do you give to a person who is a moron in geometry one day and a genius in geometry the next day?

Shredder is doing his best to irritate Kenny with this "what kind of a person" business, but Kenny is not irritated.

Kenny, as a matter of fact, is not even listening.

Up goes a hand. Of course, it's Jo-Bob Ross, the class suck.

"I think that kind of a person is the kind of a person who tries to get attention all the time because that kind of a person lacks self-esteem," says Jo-Bob.

Jo-Bob says "self-esteem" like he knows that it's a real zinger and that Shredder is mentally writing down "A" right in the middle of Jo-Bob's forehead.

Jo-Bob is a star since he did his history talk on the woman who sewed the first American flag. Her name was Betsy Ross, and Jo-Bob kept trying to say that he *thought* he was related to Betsy Ross, he wasn't sure, they had some old pictures at home that his great-grandfather had taken of the needle and thread that the famous Betsy Ross had used to sew the flag in America in 1776. He wasn't *sure* but he thought *maybe*, he, Jo-Bob Ross, was a direct descendant of the famous American Historical Heroine, Betsy Ross, who sewed the very first ever American flag in her back kitchen in Philadelphia – where Jo-Bob comes from, by the way – sewed the very first American flag with George Washington sitting right there beside her, helping her thread the needle, with just a little candle burning in the back kitchen and a black cloth over the window because, outside, the British soldiers were torturing everybody, trying to find out who the traitors were, and if anybody was caught sewing any stars or stripes on a cloth and calling it the new flag of America, of course, they would be killed instantly, and then tortured to death as well.

Shredder loved Jo-Bob Ross's speech about all this and gave him an A with about a dozen pluses behind it and it just made everybody sick.

Especially Kenny.

Jo-Bob was always talking about how American history was better than Canadian history and asking how come we didn't sing the Canadian national anthem real loud in school every morning and have the national flag on a pole at the front of the class-room like they do in Philadelphia.

Anyway, not long after the first-last business with the geometry, Jo-Bob Ross is going on and on about the country and the flag and patriotism and all that. Finally Kenny can't take it any more and tells Jo-Bob pretty loud where he can put the flagpole, which isn't a very ladylike thing to say, and Shredder hears her say this and blows up.

His way of blowing up is he starts on one of his "Perhaps a certain person" speeches.

"Perhaps a certain person who thinks she knows everything about certain topics feels she can do better herself. Perhaps a certain person who makes rude statements regarding other peoples' knowledge could offer the class the history of the flag of her own country. Perhaps that certain person will be presenting that topic to the class this coming Tuesday, or perhaps a certain person will be scoring zero, *zilch*, and *squat* in history on her next report card!"

So Kenny's got a special project to give on Canada's flag and how this project goes is what I'm going to tell you now.

So we're off to the library.

I'm going to help Kenny make the best speech about Canada's flag that's ever been. We're going to find out stuff about it that's so exciting it will make Jo-Bob's story about his so-called ancestor, Betsy Ross, and the American flag sound as boring as one of Shredder's speeches.

"And if there isn't enough exciting stuff," says Kenny, who's eyes are sparkling, "we'll make the rest of it up!"

When Kenny's eyes go funny like that, it means she's in a "be first" mood.

On the bus to the main library Kenny is talking about the first-or-last business, the all-or-nothing stuff that Shredder hates so much.

"Take that geometry, for instance," says Kenny. "That test I got the hundred in. When I was doing it, I could see everything in front of me, clear as crystal. I could see how every triangle and every rectangle fit and how all the angles made perfect sense. I felt like I was way up in the air and I could see down on the whole thing. When I'm like that, I can do anything."

Her eyes are burning while she's saying this.

Right across from us a kid with a magic marker is trying to write the names of the four turtles all over the back of the seat.

Kenny yells up to the front.

"Hey, bus driver, there's a lamebrain back here defacing public property! Hey, mister driver, there's a moron here writing with magic marker all over your bus seats! And he can't even spell Michelangelo!"

The driver is looking in his mirror. He stops the bus. He calls on his phone for a policeman or somebody. Everybody's looking around at Kenny and the kid. The kid is squirming, trying to crawl through the floor of the bus. His friend is trying to get the window open.

The driver drives to the next stop. Somebody gets out the back door and the two perps get off too.

Later, when it's time for us to get off the bus, we go to the front door instead of the back door where you're supposed to go.

We go to the front because Kenny knows something. She knows the driver will thank her for what she did and that the people on the bus will give her a round of applause.

And they do.

That Kenny, way up there, seeing it all.

There are a few books on the Canadian flag in the history section in the library, but all of them are about a flag "debate," which doesn't sound very exciting.

Was Betsy Ross "debating" with George Washington back in 1776 in her kitchen about the flag while the British soldiers were shooting traitors out in the yard?

Isn't a "debate" what you do in school when the teacher runs out of ideas?

There is one book called *Canada's Flag* by a guy named Matheson. There's a nice picture of the flag on the front, the flag curling a bit in the wind, the red maple leaf looking proud but kind of shy too, hiding a little bit. We sign that one out.

Right outside the library we get one small order of chips to share, salt and vinegar in the middle, from the chip wagon there, talk to Frenchy the chip man for a while, then grab a bus home.

On the bus, we talk some more about the first-and-last business.

"But sometimes," Kenny says, "I can't see the triangles or the rectangles at all. I can't see how anything fits anything, angles or spaces or anything. It's like I'm down on the ground, in the middle of a big crowd of strangers, lost."

Kenny, she's either way up in the air where she can see everything, or she's right on the ground, lost and blind.

Me, I'm usually partway up a hill. I can see some of it, but I can never see all of it. And I'm always in that exact same spot. It never seems to change.

Seventy-five is what I usually get.

I'm invited over to Kenny's for supper and I'm sitting there at the table watching Kenny's little dog Nerves the Ninth eat her supper on the floor beside Kenny's chair. Nerves the Ninth gets whatever the humans are eating at the time. If it's bacon and eggs and toast and tea, that's what Nerves the Ninth gets. On Christmas, Nerves the Ninth gets turkey, cranberries, stuffing, turnips, and even pie and ice cream.

I've even seen Nerves the Ninth munch away on a bowl of popcorn while the family is watching a rented movie. What a dog!

This night we're having spaghetti and meatballs and Nerves the Ninth is having a hard time with the spaghetti. The meat balls are easy but the long strings of spaghetti keep slipping out of her mouth as she tries to chew.

As you've probably noticed, dogs can't chew with their mouths closed. And they can't suck spaghetti.

Kenny's dad, who is also having some trouble with the spaghetti, is listening to Kenny and me talk about Kenny's flag assignment. Kenny's dad is dressed up as a Hydro repairman. He's got coveralls and a tool belt and a hardhat on. He's in a hurry because he has to go out on some special secret assignment.

Kenny's dad works for CSIS, the Canadian Security and Intelligence Service. He used to be a Mountie. Kenny always says that the work he does is so secret that even *he* doesn't know what it is. To-night he's disguised as a Hydro repairman. Probably going up a pole somewhere to listen in on some-body's conversation.

Kenny's mom goes to the door and kisses the Hydro repairman goodbye and comes back and sits down.

"WHAT'S THIS ABOUT THE FLAG?" says Kenny's

mom, who talks really loud. "I KNOW THE WOMAN WHO SEWED CANADA'S VERY FIRST FLAG, IF THAT'S ANY HELP TO YOU. HER NAME IS JOAN O'MALLEY. I WENT TO SCHOOL WITH HER."

Kenny's mouth drops open and so does mine. Nerves the Ninth drops a fistful of spaghetti out of her mouth back onto her plate.

"How can that be?" Kenny and I say almost both together.

Kenny's mom explains that Canada only got her own flag early in 1965. Before that, Canada's flag was always the British flag, the Union Jack.

"The Americans have had their own flag for more than two hundred years," Kenny says, and I know we're both thinking the same thing. That suck Jo-Bob Ross is going to laugh at us.

Kenny's mom explains that her friend Joan O'Malley had just moved in with her new husband – she was only twenty – and her father, who was helping them silkscreen the flag cloth over at the Exhibition Commission at the Department of Trade and Commerce, phoned his daughter up at the last minute because they needed somebody with a sewing machine to sew the flag. Kenny's mom says she was over visiting her friend Joan O'Malley on the night she was sewing it. She lived on the Baseline Road. A road that should be famous now, but it isn't.

"You were *there?*" says Kenny, her eyes going funny.

"YES, I WAS THERE — IN FACT, I THREADED THE NEEDLE IN THE MACHINE AT ONE POINT. NO BIG DEAL!" says Kenny's mom, who was trying to keep her voice down.

Imagine! We can talk to the lady who actually sewed the first flag! And Kenny's mom was there! Wait until Jo-Bob Ross hears this.

Kenny is away up there right now.

She can see it all!

Jo-Bob Ross's *mom* wasn't *there* while the *American* flag was being sewed! We're sure of that. Unless, of course, Jo-Bob's mom is over two hundred years old!

Next day Kenny and I take an 18 bus, then transfer to a 2 out to Bank Street and Walkley Road to the Cromwell Drive address, ring the bell, and the Betsy Ross of Canada opens the door. She's short and cute and doesn't weigh very much. She has brown eyes. Slacks. Sweater.

Because Kenny's mom phoned her before our visit, Joan O'Malley has the sewing machine out on the table. A Singer. Kenny and I feel the sewing machine. It feels like history.

"No big deal," she says. "Just sewed the edges and along the leaf and sewed the groove for the rope and sewed the holes for the grommets."

Did anything happen? Did anybody get arrested for

treason? Was anybody caught? Were there any enemy soldiers? Was anybody put in jail? Executed? Was there danger? Were the blinds down? Was the father of our country there? Who *is* the father of our country?

No big deal, says Joan O'Malley.

Oh yes, one thing happened.

"The thread broke once," says Joan O'Malley. "I think your mother threaded the machine for me while I put on some coffee."

"Then my dad came back and delivered it to Prime Minister Pearson's house about eleven o'clock that night. It was November 6, 1964. But the flag wasn't approved until more than a month later. So we didn't even know it was going to be our flag. It was only one of the ones being considered. There was another one, I remember, with a stupid-looking beaver on it."

On the buses going home, Kenny and I are getting more and more worried.

Nothing *happened*! Nothing very exciting anyway. Not compared to Betsy Ross and all that, back in 1776.

Kenny has that look that says she is going to come last.

At home we tell Kenny's mom about our worries and about Jo-Bob Ross.

Kenny's mom has a funny look on her face. She wants to know when exactly it is that Kenny has to do the report on the flag. At ten-thirty next Tuesday morning, Kenny tells her. We should know. It's been on Shredder's blackboard all week with "P.L.O." written all around it! Kenny's mom is up to something.

Ten-thirty next Tuesday arrives. It's time for Kenny's talk.

Just before Kenny gets up, we notice that her father is at the door. What's he doing here? She goes and talks to him. Then she comes back in, looking a little confused. Then she starts her presentation.

"My presentation on Canada's flag today involves several guests. My first guest is an undercover agent from the Canadian Security and Intelligence Service."

Kenny's dad comes in. He's wearing a Lone Ranger-type eyemask!

This isn't what Kenny's presentation was going to be! I look at Kenny. She gives me a wink. Obviously there's been some last-minute changes in the program!

Wearing the mask, Kenny's dad tells about fifteen lies about the night of November 6th, 1964.

Kenny and I can't believe our ears. Her dad spins this wild tale, involving the following items:

A Russian assassin riding up on top of the elevator in the apartment building on the Baseline Road.

Undercover agents lifting the manhole covers on the Baseline Road and dropping into the sewers. A de-fused bomb in the sewing machine. A terrorist van exploding down the road. A man tapping telephones up a pole. A woman disguised as the real Joan O'Malley who sewed the first Canadian flag. An American CIA satellite beaming signals through Joan's window. A British spy disguised as Joan's father, sent there to steal the flag.

Her dad's tale is done. He signals Kenny. Kenny gets back up.

"Our next guest is my mother, who was *there* that night and threaded the needle that sewed the flag!"

There's an *oooh!* from the class.

Then Kenny's mom comes in.

"I was there that dark and stormy night," says Kenny's mom. It's the only time I've ever heard her talk softly. It sent shivers up our backs.

She tells us a bunch of stuff how she led the enemy to the next apartment, to the fake Joan O'Malley, and then slipped through a secret door that looked like a bookcase into the real O'Malleys' apartment!

Then in comes Kenny's dad again with a short, cute woman with brown eyes who doesn't weigh very much who tells us she was the *fake* Joan O'Malley, and then the three of them go out and then Kenny's dad comes back in with Joan O'Malley again but she has a different coat on and a hat and she says she's the real Joan O'Malley! Talk about mysterious! Then Kenny's mom comes back in with the actual sewing machine!

Then they go around the room showing everybody bits of thread and the needle and the machine and Joan's disguise and spreading around more lies. Everybody's feeling the sewing machine, trying on the disguise.

Then they leave and Kenny says, "That is my Canadian flag presentation. Thank you very much for listening."

Everybody knows that this is the best presentation yet. Even Shredder says the word "excellent," but it sort of sticks in his throat.

At Kenny's that night we're happy. Too bad Kenny's dad's not there, but he's out doing something secret. The last time Kenny's mom saw him, he was dressed in a clown suit.

Kenny's mom tells us that she and Joan O'Malley used to put on shows all the time at Immaculata High School when they went there with the nuns.

Was it wrong to lie like that about the flag and about Canadian history we wonder? Not that we care much.

It's not lying, Kenny's mom tells us, it's making

things up. The nuns, she says, made up stuff all the time back at Immaculata.

Then we tell her that it was a good show and how Shredder liked it and how, best of all, it shut that suck Jo-Bob Ross right up tight.

"WAS HE THE ONE WITH THE LOOK ON HIS FACE LIKE SOMEBODY JUST HIT HIM WITH A FRESH FISH?" Kenny's mom says, back to her normal voice.

"THAT MUST HAVE BEEN HIM!" says Kenny, imitating her mom. Kenny's eyes are the eyes she has when she comes first.

And we all laugh.

And even Nerves the Ninth laughs, or at least she looks like she's laughing but, of course, there's no sound coming out.

The Liar Hunter

W.O. MITCHELL

If there is anything folks are more fussy about than
their own kids, Jake says, it is the truth. They will get
pretty snuffy if someone tells them they haven't got
any too good a grip on the truth. Jake ought to know;
sometimes he will give the truth a stretch or two, but
not like Old Man Gatenby. When Jake is done with
her she will snap back into place; with Old Gate she
is stretched for good.

Old Man Gatenby lives on his half section down
Government Road from us, him and his daughter,
Molly. He is about 40% wheat farmer, Jake says, 30%
plain liar, and 30% magnifying glass. Even so, folks
don't call him a liar. Not with the temper he's got.

Truth is a real handy thing to have lying around,

Jake says, but sometimes a little of her will go a long ways. Miss Henchbaw at Rabbit Hill says Jake makes too little go too long a ways. You would expect her to say that. She is a teacher. She wouldn't be so fussy about the truth if she had got mixed up with Mr. Godfrey last summer.

Mr. Godfrey was the fellow came out West to visit with Molly Gatenby, and it was him gave old Gate the worst dose of the truth that he ever got. Jake and me saw him the first day he was in town, because Old Man Gatenby was busy finishing up his crop and he asked us to give Mr. Godfrey a lift out from town. We did.

Without those glasses and that pale sort of a skin he had he would have been a nice-looking fellow. His eyes put me in mind of Mr. Cameron's when he goes on about the flesh being so awful and the spirit being so dandy – dark and burny. Whenever he would say anything the words came out real far apart, like flies he was picking off fly-paper. He was all the time clearing his throat just before he said something. He could have been a consolidated school principal.

He was just the kind of a fellow you would expect Molly to run with, her being so schoolteacher serious too. It is funny for Old Gate to have a daughter like Molly. Her eyes are not old-timer eyes. Her face is not all creased up like some brown paper you crumple in your hand and then try to smooth out. Her eyes will put you in mind of those violets that are tangled up in prairie grass along about the end of April.

I guess she is the violet and Old Gate is the dead grass. That's how they are.

Until we were out of Crocus, with Baldy's hind quarters tipping up and down real regular and telephone poles stretching clear to the horizon, Mr. Godfrey didn't say anything. Then he cleared his throat and said:

"The smallness of man – the prairies bring it to one with – such impact – it – is almost the catharsis of tragedy."

A jack rabbit started up to the left of the road, went over the prairie in a sailing bounce. "Huh!" Jake said.

"Catharsis – cleansing – as in the Greek tragedy – cathartic."

"Oh," Jake said, "that. Thuh alkali water sure is fear . . ."

"Oh, no," Mr. Godfrey said. "I mean that it – has a . . ."

"Prairie's scarey," I said.

"Yes." He looked down at me. "That's it – exactly it."

"I heard yuh was one of them prefessers," Jake said. He spit curvy into the breeze. "Ain't diggin' in thuh bank of thuh Brokenshell, are yuh?" He meant where they're getting those bones – the big ones that are older than anything.

"I dig," Mr. Godfrey said, "in a manner of speaking – but for folklore."

"Whut kinda ore?"

"Lore. Folklore – art – the common people . . ."

"That's real nice." Jake jiggled the lines at Baldy's rump. "Who the heck is Art an' what's this all about?"

"Why – I . . ." He cleared his throat. "I look for songs – ballads that have – that express the life of the Old West."

"'Baggage Coach Behin' the Train'?" Jake said. "'Where Do the Flies Go in the Wintertime?'"

"But – mostly stories," Mr. Godfrey said, "tall tales."

"Is that right?" Jake looked real pleased, and he cleared his throat the way he does before he starts to yarn.

"I'm looking for liars," Mr. Godfrey said.

Those dark, hungry eyes were staring right at Jake. Jake swallowed. "Yuh don't hafta look at me!"

"Sorry."

"You bin talkin' to Miss Henchbaw!"

"Do you think that she might help me? . . ."

"Her! Truthfullest woman we got aroun' here – next tuh Molly Gatenby. Why, she . . ."

"Would you consider Mr. Gatenby a good source –
of tall tales?"

"All depends," Jake said. "Anythin' Gate tells yuh,
she's blowed up to about four times natural size. You
take hailstones –"

"A chronic liar."

"Say!" Jake jumped. "Jist who do you – oh – yuh
mean Gate."

"Interesting type."

"How many kindsa liars you turned up so far?"

"There's the defensive liar – and the occasional
liar. I mentioned the chronic liar. The pragmatic or
practical liar. I'm looking for the creative liar, of
course."

"Oh – a-course," Jake said. "About Gate – I wouldn't
like tuh say he lied exactly – jist sorta deckerates thuh
truth a bit." He looked away from Mr. Godfrey's eyes.
"That's all." He looked back to Mr. Godfrey. "Tell me
somethin'. You ever run intuh any trouble with folks?"

"Not yet," said Mr. Godfrey.

"Well, young fella," Jake said, "ye're gonna."

The rest of the way home we just rolled along with
the buckboard wheels sort of grinding. A gopher
squeaked a couple of times. The way it is in fall, the air
was just like soda pop. Every once in a while would
come a tickle to your nose or your forehead, and you
would brush at it, only it would keep right on tickling.

You couldn't see the spider webs floating on the air, except where sunshine caught onto them and slid down. Mr. Godfrey had a lost look on his face whilst he stared off to the horizon with its straw-stacks curling their smoke into the soft blue sky.

At Gatenby's corner Mr. Godfrey said thanks very much, and Jake looked like he was going to say something, then he seemed to change his mind and clucked at Baldy instead. Just before we turned in, Jake said: "I kin har'ly wait fer Gate tuh come over fer rummy tuhmorra night."

But Old Gate didn't come till a week later, and when he got to our place he wasn't joking about how he'd nail Jake's hide to a fence post. All the time he played rummy he kept drumming his fingers on the kitchen table. I saw him miss the Queen of Hearts for a run and the ten of spades to make up three of a kind. Jake marked down 45 against Gate.

"Ain't doin' so smart tuhnight, Gate."

"Deal them there cards."

"Yore deal, Gate."

Gate started in shuffling the cards, all the time chewing so his chin come up almost to his nose.

Jake picked up the first card Gate dealt. "Looks like a early winter."

"Leave them cards lie till I git 'em dealt!" Gate said it real short. Then, "'Tain't polite."

Jake didn't say anything at all.

Gate lost the whole game. When Jake shoved him the cards to deal a new hand, he said:

"Tuh hell with her, Jake."

"Ain't yuh feelin' so good, Gate?"

"Feelin' good!" Gate's voice cracked. He leaned across the table. "Right now you are lookin' a teetotal nervous wreck right between the eyes!"

"Now – that's too –"

"My nerves – plum onstrung – hangin' lose as thuh fringe on a Indian jacket. I tripped in 'em three times yesterday between thuh hog pens an' thuh stock trough. An –"

"I wouldn't take on like that, Gate," Jake said. "Yuh gotta relax."

"Take on! Relax! 'Tain't no skin offa yore knuckles! 'Tain't you he's callin' a liar – in yer own house – in fronta yer own daughter!"

Jake's mouth dropped open. "Did he do that, Gate?"

"He might as well an' be done with her!"

"Either he did," Jake said, "er he didn't. Whatta yuh mean?"

"Look," Mr. Gatenby said, "he's got him a little black notebook – keeps her in his hip pocket – every time I open my mouth, he opens that there notebook! "Member thuh winter of o' six,' I sez. Out comes thuh notebook. 'Is it a fact?' he sez. 'Certain'y is,' I sez. Bang, he snaps her shet – me too. Can't git another word outa me! Like thrashin' – ready tuh roll an' he ups an' throws a ball of binder twine intuh thuh cylinders. 'Is it a fact?' he sez. Whut's he think I'm gonna tell him, thuh fat-brained, stoop-shouldered –"

"Now – ain't that cathartic."

Old Gate stared at Jake.

"New way of sayin' she's tragical," Jake said quick.

Gate grunted. "I'll tell yuh one thing fer certain – they ain't gonna be no liar hunters tied up with thuh Gatenby outfit."

He meant it.

A couple of nights later I heard Ma and my Aunt Margaret talking whilst they were giving the baby his bath. Aunt Margaret stays with us whilst her husband is in the Navy. My dad fights too; he fights for the South Saskatchewans. It is Aunt Margaret's baby.

I heard her say, "With Herbert gathering this folk-lore, she's ashamed of her own father."

"Ashamed of her father!" Ma said.

"I hope nothing comes of it," Aunt Margaret said. "It would –"

"You can let his head back now." Ma looked at Aunt Margaret whilst she wrung out the washcloth. "Molly's nobody's fool. Her heart isn't going to break in a hurry. In many ways she's her father's daughter."

"A liar, Ma?"

"She is not! Don't you dare use that word again! That wood box –"

"I already filled it."

"Help Jake with the cream then."

I told Jake all about it. I said, "There's a dustup coming over to Gatenby's, Jake."

"Is there, now?" Jake said.

"Molly isn't so fussy about Mr. Godfrey makin' out her father's a – a – what he's makin' him out to be."

"A tradegy," Jake said, "to give a Greek thuh heartburn."

But a week later Jake was laughing on the other side of his face, when the whole works came over to our place to visit. That was the night Mr. Godfrey said something about how hot it had been down East that summer.

"Hot here too," Jake said. For a minute he worked on his teeth with a sharpened matchstick and then he said. "Take thuh second week in July – tar paper on thuh roof of thuh chicken house – she all bubbled up."

"Did it really?" said Mr. Godfrey. On the chair beside him was Molly, sitting straight up like she expected something to happen, and she wanted to be ready to take off quick. Old Gate he'd hardly said anything since they came, just stared at the gas lamp in the center of the kitchen table.

"Bubbled right up," Jake said. "Noon of thuh second day, wispy sorta smoke was coming off of her."

"That a fact?"

Jake gave a little start like he'd stuck himself with the point of the matchstick. "Why – certain'y," he said.

"Herbert – please!" Molly said it the way Ma talks when she's holding in before company. I took a good look at her then, and I couldn't see where she was like Old Gate. Take her hair in that lamplight, real pretty – yellow as a strawstack with the sun lying on it. Take her mouth, the way it is so red; take her all around she is pretty as a sorrel colt. Gate is enough to give a gopher the heartburn.

"– a hawin' an' a cawin' jist as I come out," Jake was saying. "That there tar paper on thuh hen house roof was so sticky thuh dumb fool crow had got himself stuck up in it. Real comical he was – liftin' one foot an' then thuh other. Course she was kinda tragical too – that there tar was hot. Musta bin kinda painful."

"Why – that's a wonderful –"

Molly cleared her throat, sort of warning; Mr. Godfrey quit reaching for his hip pocket.

"Inside of 10 minnits," Jake went on, "a whole flocka crows was circlin' over, the way they will when they hear another in trouble, an' buhfore I knew it thuh whole roof was stuck up with crows somethin' fearful."

"Herbert!" Mr. Godfrey had his notebook out and was opening it on his knee. He didn't pay any attention to Molly and the funny look she had on her face.

"Aflutterin' an' ahollerin', with their wings aslapping – our hen house sort of liftin', an' then settlin' back agin. I headed fer thuh woodpile."

"What for, Jake?" I said.

"Ax – wasn't gonna let that hen house go without a fight. I chopped thuh roof loose from thuh uprights an' away she went. Cleared thuh peak of thuh barn an' headed south."

Molly was standing up and she was looking down at Godfrey writing away like anything. Her face looked kind of white to me. "It's about time we were going," she said real soft.

"But we've just come!" Mr. Godfrey said. "This is the sort of thing I –"

"Folklore!" Molly said it like a cuss word.

Mr. Godfrey smiled and nodded his head and turned to Jake. "How long after the first crow came did –"

"Let her go fer tuhnight," Jake said.

"Don't look now," Molly said with her voice tight,

"but I'm tired and sick of being Exhibit A for the common people. Any time you feel you can –"

"Oh, no, Molly," Mr. Godfrey said, "you don't und –"

"I'm afraid I do. These happen to be my people. They –"

"No call tuh fly off of thuh handle," Jake told her.

"A little more tact on your part, Jake, wouldn't have hurt at all!"

"Me – I didn't do nothin'. That there story –"

"Just a tall tale," Molly cut in on him, "like the thousands I've listened to all my life. I'm funny, but –"

"You shore are!" Jake said.

"There isn't any harm in them," Ma said.

"What makes it worse," Molly said, "is they have no – no point – useless – utterly senseless and – immoral!"

"I can explain what it is that –" Mr. Godfrey began.

"You've been our guest!" Molly turned on him. "Not for one minute have you stopped insinuating that my –"

"I haven't been making any –"

"You certainly have!"

"Will you let me explain?"

"It's a little late for that!"

"It shore is!" Jake was mad. "Standin' there on yer hind feet an' sayin' I'm senseless an' useless an – an' im – immortal!"

"Please, Jake." That was Ma.

I got a look at Gate, and he had a grin clear across his face.

"That story about them –"

"Was a lie, Jake Trumper! However you want –"

"Are you callin' me a liar?" Jake he was off of the wood box.

"I hate to do it," Molly said, "but you asked for it, Jake. You are the biggest . . . two-handed . . . clod-busting liar I have ever known!"

The kitchen clock ticked real loud against the silence. I could hear Jake's breath whistling in his nose.

"With one exception," Molly said. "My dad." She turned to Old Gate. "Take me home!"

I knew then what Ma meant; she is Gate's daughter all right. I felt kind of sorry for Mr. Godfrey.

I felt even more sorry for him the day me and Jake went into Crocus for Ma's groceries. He was standing beside some yellow suitcases inside of MacTaggart's, right by the door. Halfway down the counter was Molly; she stayed there.

"Hullo," Jake said. "You catchin' thuh four-ten?"

"Yes," Mr. Godfrey said.

"Sorry tuh see yuh go."

"You're alone in your sentiment."

"Huh?"

"I say – you're the only one who is."

"Oh – I wouldn't –"

"I would," Mr. Godfrey said. "I've made a mess of things, and there's no use pretending I haven't." He was staring at Jake that way I told you about. I sort of fiddled with a double-oh gopher trap hanging down from the counter. Mr. Godfrey looked past Jake to Molly by the canned tomatoes. She turned away. "I'd like to tell you something before I go."

"Shoot," Jake said.

"Somethin' fer yuh tuhday?" That was Mr. MacTaggart, who had come out from the back and was leaning across the counter to Molly.

"My work is important," Mr. Godfrey said. "I'm not just a – a liar hunter simply." He was real serious. He wasn't looking at Jake.

"Any apples in?" Molly said.

"Apples," Mr. MacTaggart said, and wrote it down with his stubby pencil, then looked up at Molly for what was next.

"What I do is important. Important as history is important." Mr. Godfrey wasn't dropping his words in relays now, but talking straight along, maybe because he was so darn serious.

"Gee!" I said, "you should hear how Jake wrassled Looie Riel an' –"

"Hold her, Kid!"

"Not the history of great and famous men," Mr. Godfrey explained, "but of the lumberjacks and section men, hotel-keepers and teachers and ranchers and farmers. The people that really count."

"And – a tin of blackstrap." Molly said it to Mr. MacTaggart, but she was looking at Mr. Godfrey. She didn't sound like she was so fussy about getting any molasses.

"Their history isn't to be found in records or in books."

"This here Ontario cheese is real nice."

"Their history is in the stories they tell – their tall tales. That's why I gather –"

"Good an' nippy."

"And a pound of cheese," Molly said.

"And I can tell you why they lie," Mr. Godfrey said.

"Anythin' else?" Mr. MacTaggart said.

"If you're interested," Mr. Godfrey said.

"That'll be nice," Jake said.

"Was there somethin' else?" Mr. MacTaggart asked.

"This is a hard country, I don't have to tell you that. There are – drouth, blizzards, loneliness. A man is a pretty small thing out on all this prairie. He is at the mercy of the elements. He's a lot like – like a –"

"Fly on a platter," I said.

"Was there somethin' else yuh wanted?" said Mr. MacTaggart.

"That's right," Mr. Godfrey said. "These men lie about the things that hurt them most. Their yarns are about the winters and how cold they are the summers and how dry they are. In this country you get the deepest snow, the worst dust storms, the biggest hailstones."

"Mebbe yuh didn't hear me –" Mr. MacTaggart said to Molly – "Was there somethin' more yuh wanted?"

"Rust and dust and hail and sawfly and cutworm and drouth are terrible things, but not half as frightening if they are made ridiculous. If a man can laugh at them he's won half the battle. When he exaggerates things he isn't lying really; it's a defence, the defence of exaggeration. He can either do that or squeal." Mr. Godfrey picked up his bags and started for the door.

"Whilst you stand there makin' up yer mind," Mr. MacTaggart said, "I'll get tuh Mrs. Totcoal's order."

"People in this country aren't squealers." Mr. Godfrey was standing in the doorway.

"You go ahead with the Totcoal Order," Molly said to Mr. MacTaggart with her eyes on Mr. Godfrey. She walked right up to him and she looked right at him. "I think I've just made up my mind."

"Hey!" yelled Mr. MacTaggart, "not right in front of –"

"Jist a new kinda hist'ry," Jake said, "gonna tickle Old Gate right up the back."

"Oh!" Molly turned around. "I'd – what are we – what about Dad! He said if Herbert ever –"

"Mr. Godfrey better come out with us," Jake said. "Don't you tell yer paw anythin' about him still bein' here. Jist say ye're invited over to our place fer tuh-night. I got me a notion." Jake leaned down and picked up Mr. Godfrey's bags. "I got me a notion about what makes Old Gate tick."

At our barn Jake told me to beat it and I did. Him and Mr. Godfrey were in there for quite a while. Me, I was wondering what made Old Man Gatenby tick. I didn't find out till that night.

Gate got quite a start when he saw Mr. Godfrey.

"Ain't you went yet?" he said.

"I – I missed the train," Mr. Godfrey said. That was his first lie, what you might call a warming-up lie. Molly's face got kind of red. Gate he settled back in his chair like he was ready for a tough evening.

"Never fergit thuh year hoppers was so bad," Jake said. "Blacked out thuh sun complete."

"This district had them terribly, I understand," Mr. Godfrey said. "Of course they weren't so big, were they?"

"Big!" Jake said. "One of 'em lit on thuh airport at Broomhead, an' a RAF fella run 100 gallons a gas intuh him afore he reelized –"

"Albin!" Mr. Godfrey said – "Albin Hobblemeyer, they called that grasshopper. I have him in my files. Three years ago he –"

"Is that a fact?" Jake said.

"They named him as soon as he set foot in the district, after a man named Hobblemeyer – squashed him to death. Matter of fact he's upset a number of the investigators digging for prehistoric remains in the bank of the Brokenshell. They're not so sure that –"

"Yuh mean – mebbe them Brokenshell bones belonged to the great great gran'daddies of that there hopper?" Jake said.

"He was that big," Mr. Godfrey said. "When he leaped, the back lash from his shanks licked up the topsoil for miles behind him and the tumbleweeds –"

"Say –" Old Gate was on the edge of his chair.

"He spit tobacco juice and smeared over an entire schoolhouse just newly painted. Naturally he caused a lot of excitement. People were worried sick. They couldn't destroy him – bullets, buckshot just bounced off his chitinous hide, and people began to wonder what it would be like when he –"

"That's a pretty feeble –" Gate started in.

"– began to lay eggs. They decided the only thing they could do would be to keep it on the hop."

"Why, Mr. Godfrey?" I asked.

"A grasshopper has to dig a hole and back into it before it can lay. It was unfortunate that there was a man in the district named – uh –"

"Dewdney," Jake said. "Wasn't there a fella name of –"

Gate, he had a funny look on his face, like a fellow wanting a swim real bad but not wanting to take the jump. "Ain't no fella name a Dewdney in Broomhead. There's Dooley – got one leg shorter than thuh other – one-an'-a-half-step Dooley."

"That was the man," Mr. Godfrey said, and Old Gate looked startled. "A very close man who had wanted to dig himself a reservoir to catch the spring run-off and couldn't bring himself to laying out the money it would cost. He couldn't resist the temptation to let the grasshopper dig it for him."

Gate's mouth dropped open and stayed that way.

"Unfortunately," Mr. Godfrey said, "Albin laid an egg."

Gate swallowed. "Tell me," he said, "jist – how – how big an egg would a hopper like that lay?"

"Quite round," Mr. Godfrey said, "and about the size of the average chicken house. Mr. – uh –"

"Dooley," Gate said kind of dazed.

"– he tried to crack it with an ax, and succeeded only in throwing his right shoulder out of joint when the ax bounced off the egg."

"I'll be –"

"He decided then to pile birch chunks around it and in that way – uh – fry it – so that it couldn't hatch. As soon as he had the wood lighted he got frantic as he thought that perhaps the heat might only speed up the hatching. So he put the fire out."

"What thuh hell did he do?" Old Gate was really interested now.

"He rounded up the district's entire supply of stumping powder. The last seen of the egg, it was headed for the States."

Old Gate's breath came out of him in one long swoosh.

"Is – that – a – fact?" He said it real weak.

Mr. Godfrey was looking over at Molly, and she was smiling. Jake looked like he'd just thrashed a 60-bushel crop, too.

It was a week later, after Mr. Godfrey had gone back to stay with Gatenbys, that I asked Jake about something that had bothered me ever since that night.

"Jake," I said, "he never told what happened to that hopper."

"There," Jake said, "is thuh tragical part of it. Albin, he fell in love."

"Fell in love!"

"Yep. He was settin' in this here Dooley's back 40 one day an' he looked up an' seen one a them there four-engine bombers they're flyin' tuh Roosia. She was love at first sight. He took off, an' thuh last folks seen was two little black specks disappearin' tuh thuh North. Han' me that there manure fork will yuh, Kid?"

ABOUT THE CONTRIBUTORS

DAVID BOOTH has contributed significantly to Canadian children's literature as an editor, educator, and lecturer. He claims that "you can sometimes taste the words of a poem on your tongue as you make meaning in your imagination." "Mary Had a Little Lamb" appeared in *Doctor Knickerbocker and Other Rhymes, A Canadian Collection* (Toronto: Kids Can Press Ltd., 1993).

MAX BRAITHWAITE was born and brought up in Saskatchewan. He wrote radio plays, magazine articles, screenplays, and twenty-five books. Throughout his career, he won numerous awards, including the Stephen Leacock Award for Humour in 1972. He died in March 1995. *Never Sleep Three in a Bed* was first published in Great Britain (London: George

Allen and Unwin Ltd., 1970) and is reprinted with permission from Aileen Braithwaite.

LORNE BROWN was born in Toronto and loves to tell stories even more than to write them. He has performed widely throughout Canada. When not reading, writing, or telling stories, he can usually be found in the chimney corner, picking his banjo and singing old ballads and blues. Stories he has written appear in *Appleseed Quarterly, the Canadian Journal of Storytelling.* "Tales from the Negro Leagues" appeared in *Tales for an Unknown City,* collected by Dan Yashinsky (McGill-Queen's University Press, 1990) and is reprinted with permission from the author.

ROCH CARRIER has enjoyed a prestigious career as educator, academic administrator and consultant, serving as advisor to the Quebec Department of Cultural Affairs and as the first writer to head the Canada Council. He is one of Quebec's most popular lecturers and readers and has more than thirty books to his credit, including the recently published *The Basketball Player* (Toronto: Tundra Books, 1996). "The Hockey Sweater" was originally published in *The Hockey Sweater and Other Stories* (trans. Sheila Fischman, Toronto: House of Anansi Press Limited, 1979) and is reprinted with permission of the publisher in association with Stoddart Publishing Co. Limited, Don Mills, Ontario.

BRIAN DOYLE's roots are in the Gatineau Hills to the north of Ottawa, where his love for the spoken language was instilled by his father, who had a great knack for storytelling. He has won numerous awards, including both the Vicky Metcalf Award and the Mr. Christie Book Award in 1991. "Kenny's Canadian History" was written especially for *Laughs*.

SARAH ELLIS was born and educated in Vancouver, and worked as a music and dance critic before she became a writer. As a child, she read every day and states "My father was, and is, a good joke teller, and I think that's why I like funny books." In 1991 she was awarded the Governor General's Literary Award for *Pick-Up Sticks* (Toronto: Groundwood Books, 1994) and is currently a librarian and writer. This is the original publication of "A Palace for Aberbog."

MARTYN GODFREY was born in England and moved to Canada when he was eight. He lived in Toronto and "created my first real character in grade seven." He went on to become a teacher and, as the author of numerous books and stories, has received four literary awards, including the Vicky Metcalf Short Story

Award. He wrote "The Day of the Raisin" especially for this collection.

ALICE KANE is one of Canada's greatest storytellers. Born in Ireland, she moved with her parents to Canada at the age of thirteen. For many years she was an influential children's librarian with the Toronto Public Library. After her retirement in 1973, she taught Children's Literature and began a second career as a professional storyteller.

GORDON KORMAN was born in Montreal and grew up in Toronto. He jumped into publishing at the age of fourteen with his first book *This Can't Be Happening at Macdonald Hall*. Gordon Korman graduated in Dramatic and Visual Writing from New York University and, when he's not writing, spends part of each year visiting students throughout North America. "A Reasonable Sum," copyright © 1989 by Gordon Korman, is from *Connections: Short Stories*, Donald R. Gallo, Editor. Used by permission of Delacorte Press, a division of Bantam Doubleday Dell Publishing Group, Inc.

DENNIS LEE was born in Toronto. He was seven when his first poem was published in a children's magazine. In addition to poetry, his unique way with words led him to writing song lyrics, including the words for most of the songs in the television series "Fraggle Rock." He has published numerous books of poetry and received many prestigious awards, including the Order of Canada in 1994. "The Sitter and the Butter and the Better Batter Fritter" is from *Alligator Pie* (Toronto: Macmillan of Canada, 1974). Copyright ©1974 Dennis Lee. With permission of the author.

LORIS LESYNSKI is a graphic designer, writer, and illustrator who loves the song and dance of words. She lives in the country where she can practice her poems as loudly as she wants out in the garden. In addition to designing and illustrating the cover for this book, Loris Lesynski has given permission for her poems, "I Hate Poetry" and "Worn Out," to appear for the first time in this collection.

JEAN LITTLE was born in Taiwan and was educated at the University of Toronto. Almost blind since birth, Jean developed a love of books and a sense of escape through reading and writing. Her first poems were published in *Saturday Night* magazine when she was just seventeen, and her first novel, *Mine for Keeps*, was published in 1961. She uses a talking computer to write, and her books have been translated into many languages and have won several awards. "The Grade Five Lie" is from *Little by Little* by Jean Little. Copyright © Jean Little, 1987. Reprinted by permission of Penguin Books Canada Limited.

CLAIRE MACKAY was born in Toronto "in a little second-floor flat above a pool hall." She read voraciously as a child, but did not begin her writing career until she wrote a story called *Mini-Bike Hero* to entertain her 11-year-old son. Since then, she has written numerous books, including *Bats About Baseball* with her longtime friend, Jean Little. Claire wrote the poem "Trivial Pursuit" especially for this anthology and selected all the stories, jokes, and poems for your enjoyment because she loves to laugh.

W.O. MITCHELL was born in Saskatchewan. He has had a varied career including that of gifted teacher, visiting professor at the University of Windsor, and creative writing instructor at the Banff Centre. He is the author of many successful books, including the beloved *Who Has Seen The Wind*, and two collections of short stories, *Jake and the Kid* and *According to Jake and the Kid*. "The Liar Hunter" is from *Jake and the Kid* by W.O. Mitchell, copyright © 1961. Reprinted with permission of Macmillan Canada and the author. All rights reserved.

L.M. MONTGOMERY was born and brought up in Cavendish, Prince Edward Island. She started writing poetry at the age of nine and stories at eleven. In 1908, her first novel, *Anne of Green Gables*, became an instant best-seller and she went on to publish many, many more. In 1911, she moved to a small Ontario town when she married Reverend Ewan Macdonald and continued writing until her death in 1942. "Diana Is Invited to Tea with Tragic Results" is from *Anne of Green Gables* – the famous novel that has been translated into seventeen languages and continues to be loved worldwide.

BILL RICHARDSON, the self-appointed poet laureate of Canada, was born and brought up in Winnipeg, Manitoba, and now lives in Vancouver, British Columbia. He is a writer and broadcaster, working principally with CBC Radio. He is the author of several books, and won the Stephen Leacock Award for Humour in 1994 for *The Bachelor Brothers' Bed and Breakfast*. "Soothing the Savage Beast" is from *Come Into My Parlour*, written by Bill Richardson, reprinted with the permission of Polestar Book Publishers Ltd., 1011 Commercial Drive, Vancouver, BC, V5L 3X1.

KEN ROBERTS was born in Florida and attended both the University of California and McMaster

University in Hamilton, Ontario. He became a children's librarian and has worked as both a storyteller and puppeteer, traveling across the country. He started writing stories in 1981, and his first novel, *Pop Bottles*, was published in 1987. He now combines a writing career with his position as CEO of the Hamilton Public Library. "Gross" is an original story written especially for this anthology.

RICHARD SCRIMGER has written several novels, one of which, *Crosstown*, was published this year to wide critical acclaim – he doesn't know exactly how wide, but it was wide. His humorous short fiction appears in magazines and newspapers, and a collection entitled *Still Life with Children* is scheduled for publication in the summer of 1997. Richard lives with his wife and four children in Cobourg, Ontario, and wrote "Introducing Norbert" expressly for this book.

LOIS SIMMIE is a Saskatchewan-born author who grew up on the prairies, married, raised four children and worked at various jobs before beginning her writing career. She has written successfully for both adults and children who particularly love her books of nonsense verse. She often collaborates with her daughter, illustrator Anne Simmie, and knows that humor appeals to children immensely. "Jimmy Lorris" is from *Who Greased the Shoelaces?* by Lois Simmie (Toronto: Stoddart Publishing Co. Limited, 1989), and "My Little Brother" is reprinted from *An Armadillo Is Not a Pillow* by Lois Simmie, published by Douglas & McIntyre, copyright © 1986. Reprinted with permission.

TIM WYNNE-JONES was born in England, but spent his early childhood in British Columbia before moving to Ottawa. He studied architecture and fine art, but turned to writing full-time with the publication of his adult novel, *Odd's End.* He has won many literary awards, including the Governor General's Literary Award in 1993 for *Some of the Kinder Planets,* and in 1995 for *The Maestro.* "The Clark Beans Man" is from *The Book of Changes,* copyright © 1994 by Tim Wynne-Jones. A Groundwood Book/Douglas & McIntyre. Reprinted by permission of Orchard Books, New York.